Falmouth Thirteen

Falmouth Thirteen

Supernatural Tales From A Cornish Town

Evie Payne

For Mum

Table of Contents

Acknowledgements

Thanks to all the individuals who helped to make this book happen. The people I met and worked with on the Cornwall Adult Education Creative Writing courses and subsequent critique sessions. The kind volunteers at the Falmouth History Archive, at The Poly, for their knowledge of Falmouth and access to the huge collection of historical documents and photos. Special thanks to Ella Walsworth-Bell for her feedback, suggestions and ongoing support, and her family for welcoming me into their home on Wednesday evenings. Special thanks also, to Kath Morgan for her tuition, guidance, editing, insight and vast knowledge of the writing craft. Most of all, thanks to my wife, Benita, for her patience and understanding during the creation of this book and for her endless love that makes everything worthwhile.

The Black Rock Revenant

I was nine years old when I first saw him. Christmas Eve, 1972. Dad and I went out for a drive while Mum stayed home and prepared the food for the next day's Christmas dinner.

It was a wild, stormy day. Along Falmouth's main street, the Christmas lights strung between the shops swayed and bounced, hammered by the wind. Most of the shops were closed by late afternoon, but the window displays were still lit up. I peered at the festive items in the shop windows, and wished hard that Santa would bring me all I wanted.

As we passed a shop window with a huge stack of wrapped presents, I saw a hand reach down and grab the top present.

'Dad, Dad. Did you see that?'

'See what Jack, my boy?'

I told him what I had seen.

He laughed. 'Another one of your tall tales? Jack-anory, tell a story.'

I knew better than to bother arguing.

'Shall we have a look and see how rough it is up at the Point, Jack?'

As we approached the car park at Pendennis Point, I could see the spray that blew up from the waves crashing on the rocks below. The car shook with the force of the wind as Dad parked up at the seaward end of the car park, facing the oncoming weather. Clouds of grey and black raced towards us, driven by the south-westerly wind. I asked if I could get out of the car and watch the waves.

'Wait there, son, I'll come and open the door for you.'

Dad struggled to open his door, straining against the wind. He came around, opened my door, and I jumped out. As I moved out of the shelter of the door, the wind nearly blew me over. The air was biting cold and heavy with the smell of salt water and rotting seaweed. I heard a deep thud as a wave smashed onto the rocks, followed by a huge curtain of spray that shot up high and blew way over my head. I turned to follow its progress, then broke into a run to see if it would land in the sea on the other side of the point. I heard Dad call my name, so I stopped at the kerb in time to see the spray almost make it to the water. I was about to head back to the car, when I looked out to the Black Rock beacon in the middle of the estuary: a massive cone made of granite blocks and topped off with a huge spherical iron cage mounted on a pole. As my gaze was drawn from the cage down to a big wave that slammed into the side of the beacon, my jaw dropped in shock. A figure. A man. Stood on the leeward side of the conical beacon. He wore dark coloured clothing and waved a stick above his head as if to attract attention. I felt my heartbeat quicken as I turned and tried to run to Dad, but the wind blew so hard I could barely make any progress.

'Dad! There's someone out there on the rocks.'

The strong south-westerly stole the words from my mouth and rushed them away to the north-east. Dad was stood next to our red Hillman Minx car, looking out to sea. I glanced back towards Black Rock as I ran. The dark clad figure was still there. I stumbled and my heart skipped a beat, then beat faster. I managed to stop myself from falling, and as I picked up my pace again, Dad turned to face me.

'Everything all right, Jack?' he said, a concerned look upon his face.

'There's a man, out on Black Rock,' I said pointing behind me.

Dad looked out to the beacon. 'Surely not in this weather?'

'There is, there is, honest,' I said, turning.

As we looked across the half mile to Black Rock, a huge wave crashed against the cone of the beacon and obscured the view of the rocks around the base for a few seconds. When the rocks were visible again, no figure was to be seen.

'I can't see him,' I said.

'Are you sure this isn't one of your tall tales?'

'He was really there, on the left of the marker-cone thingy. He was waving a stick above his head, like this.' I raised my right arm over my head and waved it from side to side.

I think Dad could tell by the distressed tone of my voice that I was serious.

'Probably washed off by one of those waves. Let's see if there's anyone in the Coastguard station down below. Better let someone know about it.'

As we made our way across the car park, it started pelting with rain. A gust of wind blew us sideways, as if deliberately trying to impede our progress. Dad put his arm around me, his fingers curled firmly and protectively over my shoulder. The late afternoon daylight seemed to grow darker with every step as we headed down to the Coastguard station.

I could hear the waves boom as they smashed against the rocks on the windward side of the headland. Spray from the impact was caught by the wind and lifted up and over the cliff, straight into Dad and I. The icy-cold spray burned my face and made my eyes sting. I gasped in shock; water entered my mouth and nostrils, the salty tang causing a tingling sensation.

The wires and ropes on the flagpole next to the coastguard hut whistled and whined in the wind. Light streamed out from the glass fronted lookout station. Dad steered us along the back of the building to a door on the sheltered side, and knocked hard. The door swung open to reveal a figure silhouetted by the light inside. I could just make out an old man with a wispy beard, a woolly hat pulled down over his ears.

'Af'noon,' said the man, 'Come on in out the rain.'

Dad ushered me into the hut and the man closed the door behind us. The inside of the hut was warm and bright, a stark contrast to the cold and gloom outside. The room smelt of Paraffin fumes and tea. A younger man sat next to a paraffin heater, in front of a huge window that looked out over the bay. An empty chair stood to the other side of the heater.

'All right chaps.' The younger man smiled and nodded his head in greeting.

The older man walked past me and Dad, then turned to face us. 'That there's Davey Nancholas, and I'm Bill Trewen. Now, how can we help 'ee?'

I noticed the brown, timeworn skin on the small area visible between Bill's beard and his hat.

Dad put his hands on my shoulders. 'Jack reckons he saw someone out on Black rock.'

'Did 'ee indeed?' Bill looked at me, then glanced over his shoulder. 'Davey, have a gander over at Black Rock will 'ee?'

'On it, boss,' Davey said. He picked up the biggest pair of binoculars I had ever seen, and aimed them towards Black Rock.

'Now tell us what happened, young Master Jack?' Bill said.

I drew my eyes away from the binoculars and back towards Bill. I noticed the look on his face, eyes open wide and mouth a fixed grin. I knew that look. I'd seen the same look on Dad's face when he thought I was telling one of my 'tall tales'. Bill didn't believe me, but I recounted what had happened anyway. When I'd finished, Bill turned to look at Davey, who gave a quick shake of his head.

When Bill looked back, I noticed his expression changed, the fixed grin became feigned concern. The eyes narrowed, but I could see the mirth in them.

'Right then,' Bill said. 'Could be he's still out there but we can't see him in the fading light, or he's possibly been swept off by the waves. So 'ere's what I suggest; Davey and I will keep an eye out, and if we see him, then the lifeboat

4

will be summoned quicker than you can say "Cornish clotted cream". How does that sound?'

I knew there was no point in arguing. 'That sounds like the best idea, Sir, thank you.'

'Thank you, for taking the time to let us know. I wish you a very happy Christmas.'

Dad returned the courtesy and we left the hut. It was full dark outside and the storm raged around us, so we hurried back to the car. Once inside, Dad started the engine and said, 'Better get back and tell your Mum what's happened. She's probably wondering where we've gotten to.'

I was angry that Bill didn't believe me, but as Dad and I made our way home, the anger was replaced by a question: who was the man out on Black Rock? As the years went by, I often pondered the question of who it was I saw. Every time I saw Black Rock, I looked for the figure and thought about that Christmas Eve.

Eleven years later, I was home from University for the Christmas holidays and was sat at the breakfast table with Mum and Dad on the Friday after Christmas. I munched on toast, slathered with butter, whilst I skimmed through the local newspaper. I was about to skip the page about Shipping News, when an article at the bottom caught my attention.

Inshore Lifeboat launched on Christmas Eve.
Falmouth Inshore lifeboat launched at 15.30pm on Christmas Eve following reports of a man stranded on the rocks at Black Rock Beacon in the Carrick Roads. A family visiting Pendennis Point raised the alarm. They reportedly saw a figure in dark clothing waving what appeared to be a stick. The lifeboat search was carried out around Black Rock but nothing was found. The search was abandoned after an hour due to worsening weather. The Lifeboat returned safely to port at 17.15pm.

I sat there, mouth open, the piece of toast I was about to bite into forgotten. I tried to read the article again, but my eyes didn't register the words due to my brain going into overdrive.

'You okay, Jack?' Mum said. 'You look like you've seen a ghost.'

Hot butter ran off the toast onto my hand, then dripped onto the newspaper.

'Jack, your Mother is talking to you.'

'Uh...sorry Mum.'

'You're white as a sheet,' Mum said. 'And you've dripped butter all over the paper. Neither your Dad nor I have read it yet.'

'Sorry. Listen to this.' I read out the newspaper article. When I had finished, there were a few moments silence. I looked at my parents. Mum wore a frown. Dad's eyebrows were raised in surprise.

'Curious,' he said. 'Any more toast?'

'Probably just a coincidence,' Mum said.

'A man, waving a stick, on Black Rock on Christmas Eve? That's exactly what I saw, Mum. Dad?'

'Maybe it's Santa getting ready for the big night,' Dad said, laughing.

I felt my body tense. 'Don't be ridiculous, Dad. I know what I saw, even if you don't believe me.'

There were a few moments of uncomfortable silence, then Mum said, 'I saw Lucy Harvey yesterday, Jack.'

'Really,' I replied, not interested.

'She asked after you.'

'Great.' I pretended to stifle a yawn.

Mum stood up and started clearing the breakfast dishes. 'She's turned out to be a lovely young lady. Remember when the two of you used to play together?'

I let out an exasperated sigh. 'That was when I was in junior school, Mum. I haven't spoken to her in years.'

'Still, maybe you should ask her out for a date?'

I stood up. My chair grated on the lino as it shot backwards. 'Yeah. Tell you what, I'll ask her if she wants to go to Castle Point and look for the man on Black Rock, shall I?'

'Jack, don't be like that,' Mum said, as I headed out of the room.

'Jack, come back here and apologise to your Mother.'

I grabbed my coat from the banister, opened the front door and stormed out, slamming the door behind me. I headed towards town, my mind swirling with questions. Why did the man only appear at Black Rock on Christmas Eve? Who was he? What did he want? How did he get there?

I resolved to find out and prove my doubting Father wrong.

When I got to town, I went into Falmouth library. It had been one of my favourite places since Mum first took me there when I learned to read. The grand staircase in the entrance hall, the huge pictures on the wall, and the grandfather clock in the corner, were all awe inspiring to me as a young boy. But the best thing was the smell of thousands and thousands of books.

I scanned the Cornwall History shelves for books on shipwrecks around the Cornish coast. I found three and carried them to the reading room and scoured through them, trying to find any references to shipwrecks around Falmouth on Christmas Eve. After an unsuccessful hour, I returned the books to the shelf and asked one of the librarians if there was any other information about shipwrecks available. The librarian told me there was a newspaper archive down the corridor with editions going back to the mid 1800's.

I entered the archive room, looked around and stopped mid-stride. My face fell at the sight of rack after rack of papers hung next to each other like books on a shelf. It would take ages to trawl through them all.

I looked at the first one on the rack; Lake's Falmouth Packet & Cornwall Advertiser, January 2nd, 1858. I scanned the front page as I pondered what to do. My eyes passed over the date again and an idea came to me. Any events on Christmas Eve would be reported just after Christmas, or in the New Year. I just had to search through those editions. I took the first newspaper off the rack, placed it on a table and searched through. It was in the 1865 New Year edition that I eventually found what I was looking for.

Ship wrecked on Black Rock. All lives lost.

The Dutch clipper "Zeelandt" sank after running aground on rocks around the Black Rock Beacon during adverse weather conditions late in the afternoon on Christmas Eve. The vessel was carrying a cargo of timber from Rotterdam to Falmouth. The Captain's name was Van Gerritsen. A semi-conscious cabin boy was washed ashore near Pendennis Point but died shortly afterwards. No other survivors were found or bodies recovered. Most of the cargo was salvaged after being washed ashore around the estuary.

Captain Van Gerritsen. Was that the man I saw out on Black Rock?

Somehow, I knew it was.

I took the newspaper to the librarian and she kindly photocopied the article for me. I headed home, a smug grin on my face. Now I had proof, Dad would have to believe me.

When I got home, Dad was in the front room watching the telly. Mum was pottering in the kitchen. I went into the kitchen and gave her a hug.

'Sorry for earlier, Mum.'

'It's okay, Jack. All forgotten now. Dinner will be ready soon.'

'Great,' I said, then went into the front room. Dad looked up at me. I didn't speak, just handed him the article from the archive. He read it then handed it back.

'Interesting. All lives lost. No survivors,' he said.

I could have screamed.

'Fine,' I said.

I walked out, went to my room and pondered Captain Van Gerritsen. I now knew who he was and how he got there. I figured he only appeared on Christmas Eve because that was the anniversary of his ship being wrecked. The answers to why he appeared and what he wanted still remained to be found.

Though I was diligent in my attendance at Castle Point every Christmas Eve, it was another four years before I saw the Captain again. The conditions were just like the first time I saw him, driving wind and rain from the southwest and a low tide. I had a feeling this was significant and made a mental note to investigate. I had brought a camera and binoculars with me, determined to get more evidence to prove the Captain's existence to Dad, as well as to satisfy my own interest. Looking through the binoculars, I made something out. Something that looked like it could be a black tricorn hat. I pulled the binoculars away from my face like they'd bitten me. Rubbed my eyes. Refocused the glasses.

There. No mistaking it. A Black tricorn hat, a long dark coat, a stick. The stick waved and I almost dropped the binoculars. My heart beat so fast I could scarcely catch my breath.

It was him. He was real. I was right and Dad was wrong.

I calmed down enough to take some photos and, after Christmas, took the film to Boots the Chemist for developing. Most of the photos revealed nothing, due to the heavy rain and poor light on the day, but one showed the vague shape of a figure with an arm raised.

I showed Dad the photo.

He snorted and said, 'At last, conclusive evidence of Santa on Black Rock.'

I knew there was no point in showing Mum. She was never happy with my 'unhealthy interest' in the Captain. Thought I was meddling with things I shouldn't, and no good would come of it. Reckoned I would be better of trying to find a nice girl to marry and start a family.

Undeterred, I researched the weather and tides for Christmas Eve 1983, when the other family had seen the Captain. It confirmed my thoughts. The Captain only appeared when the conditions were the same as the day his ship was wrecked; a south-westerly storm and a low, mid-afternoon tide, so the rocks on Black Rock were uncovered.

To try and find out more about the Captain and the Zeelandt shipwreck I started scouring local, historical records. Over a period of several weeks, I paid many visits to the newspaper archives in the library, checking out every issue for the two-week period after Christmas. When this tactic failed, I took to searching through documents in the Falmouth History Archive at the Poly.

Hours of trawling through the vast collection finally paid off when I came across a letter that appeared to be a response to a Mr Tremarnock from Lord Portminster regarding the loss of the Captain's ship, the Zeelandt.

The Chambers,

St James,

Street,

London.

January 7th, 1866

Dear Mr Tremarnock,

I am writing with regard to your letter of the 27th December. The loss of the Zeelandt and her crew is a very troubling and tragic occurrence, made doubly so by the information you have ascertained and informed me of about the events of that day. I am greatly appreciative of your efforts to salvage the majority of the timber the Zeelandt was carrying. Your swift deployment of the salvage team has turned what would have been a major financial loss into, if not a profit, at the very least a financially acceptable situation. You have my gratitude.

Yours Sincerely,
Lord Charles Portminster

Although the letter mainly referred to the salvage operation, the comments about the event left me desperate to know more. A trip to Falmouth library and a check through the most recent Who's Who book showed that the Portminster peerage still existed and the descendants of Lord Portminster lived on an estate in Buckinghamshire. I wrote to them to enquire if there was an archive that contained the original letter to Lord Portminster from Mr Tremarnock. To my surprise, a few weeks later, I received a reply that included a photocopy of Mr Tremarnock's letter.

Grove Place,
Falmouth,
27th December, 1866

Dear Lord Portminster,

It is with a heavy heart that I must inform you of a most tragic situation that occurred on Christmas Eve last. I was awaiting the arrival of the clipper, the Zeelandt. The ship, captained by Van Gerritsen, was carrying a cargo of timber ordered by the company. It was late afternoon when I received word from a member of the work crew at the Docks, who were tasked with unloading the vessel, that the ship had run aground on the Black Rock Beacon. Upon hearing the news, I despatched three tenders to row out to the stricken vessel and a land crew to make haste to the Pendennis headland. I rode out to the point and arrived just as the vessel broke apart and sank. I ordered the land crew to spread out along the water's edge and look out for survivors. The tenders took some time to arrive as they were fighting against a strong wind, a large swell, and an incoming tide. They valiantly scoured the area looking for survivors, but none were to be found in the fast fading daylight. I called off both the sea and land search and was about to depart when a body was spotted just offshore. Two men bravely swam out and recovered a young boy, probably the ship's cabin boy, from the water. The boy had sustained injuries and was barely conscious. He kept repeating the words "Kapitein gek" until sadly he passed away, despite numerous attempts to revive him. By this time, it was full dark, and I ordered everyone to stand down with a request to resume the search at first light. The following morning, Christmas Day, a large group of men, women and children assembled to assist with the search for survivors. Thankfully, the weather conditions were much improved, so the men were able to set out in various boats to search the harbour and beyond. The women and children now spread around the estuary and outer harbour. I ordered a barge to collect the timber and bring it to our yard at the Docks. By sunset, all but a small amount of timber was recovered.

There are three matters regarding the loss of the "Zeelandt" that have me perplexed. Firstly, despite searching all day, no survivors were found, nor bodies recovered. Secondly, as the vessel sank, I noticed that all sails were unfurled, a very unusual circumstance for a vessel entering harbour, particularly in such appalling conditions. Finally, and most disturbingly, the final words spoken by the cabin boy, "Kapitein gek", were later translated by a visiting Dutch sailor as, "Captain insane". My Lord, I am not one for speculation, but this whole affair has left me feeling deeply perturbed.

Yours Sincerely,

Richard Tremarnock

A shiver ran down my spine as I read the final paragraph.

Although the letter gave me details about what happened, it didn't give me any answers, only more questions. Why were no bodies recovered? A ship of that size must have had a large crew. With the wind and tide both heading onshore at least one body should have been washed ashore in the estuary. Also, why did the cabin boy say the Captain was insane? What did the Captain do to deserve such a description?

I had to know.

There was only one way to find out - go out to Black Rock and ask the Captain.

I needed a boat.

I decided the most appropriate vessel for my needs would be a rigid inflatable boat or RIB; a big rubber dinghy with a fibreglass hull. I found a 12-foot RIB for sale locally, purchased it and had the keel reinforced with stainless steel to make it as 'rock-proof' as possible. I spent many hours getting to know Black Rock. I visited it at various tides from high to low and in many different weather conditions, starting with fine and calm through to stormy. I even practised landing on it. At very low tides there was a natural inlet between the rocks on the north-east side. Using a four-pronged anchor wedged between the exposed rocks to moor up, I landed and explored. The ground was treacherous underfoot; seaweed covered deep clefts in the rocks that could easily cause a broken ankle. Before long, I knew Black Rock better than anyone else ever had.

All I needed was a Christmas Eve with the right conditions for the Captain's appearance. That came eight years later in 1995.

Falmouth harbour was grey from sea to sky as I guided the RIB between empty mooring buoys and out towards the docks. A seagull hovered overhead, manoeuvring effortlessly in the blustery wind, its call a cry of warning, imploring me to turn back. As my boat rounded Falmouth docks, Black Rock came into view. A shudder of anticipation ran through me.

The boat heaved and rocked in the turbulent swell and I struggled to keep it on course. The cold rain stung my face and hands as it blew into the exposed mouth of the estuary. From fifty yards away, I made out the individual blocks of granite that formed the cone of the beacon. At the base, a figure: The Captain. Stood with legs braced apart and both hands on his walking stick, which was planted firmly in front of him.

Waiting, I thought. Waiting for me? A knot formed in my stomach. For the first time, I questioned the wisdom of my obsession with the Captain. I swallowed a lump in my throat.

I manoeuvred the boat to the entrance of the inlet, slowing the engine to ease forward against the pull of the current. The wind and waves were comparatively calm on the leeward side of the beacon. I grabbed the anchor and cast it ashore, the painter rope flowing out behind it, then pulled the rope back towards me until two of the prongs wedged themselves in a fissure, about ten feet from the bow. With the painter secured and the engine switched off, I clambered over the side. I kept my focus on the precarious ground in front of me as I made my way towards the Captain.

Worn leather boots came into view. I stopped. Looked up. There he stood, staring at me. The stick in his hands. Only it wasn't a stick. It was a rapier sword, blackened and tarnished.

With blood?

He wore a threadbare coat, and beneath that, a dirty, stained shirt. Long, tangled black hair hung down from beneath his battered tricorn hat. A wispy, ragged beard edged his face. Wrinkles lined his dark, timeworn skin. His mouth formed a thin-lipped slit. His expression appeared neutral, but his eyes. Oh, his eyes. The depth and darkness within them induced a cold dread within me.

'Captain Van Gerritsen?'

When he replied, his voice was deep, with a heavy Dutch accent. 'I am Lars Van Gerritsen'

'My name is Jack. Good to meet you, at last.'

'Are we acquainted?'

'No, Sir, but I have seen you before. From over there.' I pointed to the Pendennis headland.

He scowled, gripped his sword in one hand and pointed it at me. 'Why have you not come before now?'

I stepped backwards. 'I haven't had the chance. You're only here when the conditions are right.'

'I am always here.'

'No, Sir. You only appear on Christmas Eve when the tide and weather are the same as the day the Zeelandt was wrecked.'

He didn't reply immediately - just stared at me. His eyes burnt into me as he searched for the truth of my words. I had never felt so vulnerable and exposed. He lowered his sword.

'Why have you come?' he said.

'To get some answers.'

'What answers?'

'What happened to the crew of the Zeelandt?'

'I killed them during the voyage. Threw their bodies overboard.'

'Why?'

'Cowardice and mutiny. The cowards wanted to turn back during the storm and return to port. When I refused, they mutinied, but they were no match for my sword.'

'Captain, you've been here for nearly a hundred and fifty years. Why?'

'Is it really so long?' He looked off into the distance for a few moments, then back at me. 'I am here to suffer for my sins, to repent.'

'For the people you killed?'

'Murder is the worst of my crimes; there are many others.'

I pondered his words then asked my final question. 'What do you want?'

He spread his arms wide. 'Release. An end to this existence.'

'How?'

'I need you to kill this body and set me free.'

'Kill you?'

'Will you do it? Will you give me release?' He deftly shifted his grip from sword handle to blade, then proffered the hilt to me. I took a step back and raised my hands defensively.

16

'I-I don't think I can.'

'Coward,' he snarled, pure hate in his eyes. He returned his grip to the sword handle.

'I've never killed anyone before.'

'Then you are no use to me.'

He raised the sword above his head and swung it towards me.

I dove to my right and landed hard on the rocks. Winded, I struggled to breathe. I had to get back to my boat and away from this madman. The words 'Capitain gek' went round and round in my head. I turned to see where he was. The Captain was headed towards the boat. Was he trying to escape? I clambered to my feet, struggling to find purchase on the slippery seaweed. I started towards the Captain. He had nearly reached the boat when he raised his sword and slashed the through the anchor rope. It parted with a twang. The boat shot backwards, pulled by the current.

'No!' I screamed.

He turned and sauntered towards me, sword raised. I stopped and looked around, in desperation. There. The anchor. Still wedged in the rocks, a few feet away from me. I leapt over to it, bent down, grabbed the shaft with both hands and pulled. The anchor rose up just in time to block the arc of the Captain's sword. Sparks flew as the two metals clashed. The captain pulled back his sword for another strike. The anchor between us. Without thinking I drove the prong upwards. Flesh squelched and bone cracked as the prong went in behind his jaw and emerged beneath his eye.

He dropped his sword, staggered backwards, then fell. The anchor yanked from my grasp. His hat flew off as he hit the ground. Guttural growls and blood flowed from his mouth. I watched in disbelief as he grabbed the anchor shaft and pulled. He had six inches of steel impaled in his head; he should be dead. The anchor emerged with a sucking sound.

Anger rose in me. I had devoted most of my life to this man and now I was going to die for my efforts?

The Captain's sword lay on the rocks at my feet. I bent down and grabbed the hilt. The Captain cast the anchor away and sat up. I roared, stepped towards him and swung the sword with both hands. It bit deep into the Captain's neck, knocking him sideways. Blood erupted from the gaping wound. He crawled away from me, heading towards the sea. I strode after him and hacked at his neck with all the strength I could muster. The force carried the blade right through. I snarled in victory as I watched his head disappear into the rough sea and his body collapse onto the rocks.

Dead.

As I gazed down at his lifeless body, I saw movement from the corner of my eye. A huge wave rose up and broke over the rocks. I dove towards the shelter of the granite cone. I landed hard and felt something break inside me as the wave roared past. Pain exploded in my chest. I turned to see the Captain's body washed into the tempestuous water and sink out of sight.

With the sword still in hand, and every movement agony, I pulled myself up until I was sat against the cold granite. My body shivered as I took in the view of the estuary, the last thing I would see in this life. I chuckled at the irony; I had survived the Captain's sword only to die from hypothermia.

Across the water, Pendennis Point was silhouetted in the last of the daylight. A figure stood up in the car park. It looked small. A child. I fought the pain and pulled myself up the beacon, using the sword for support. I leant against the granite, raised the sword and waved it above my head. The figure waved back then moved away, but soon returned with a second, taller figure.

Hope.

As I lowered the sword, I saw "Van Gerritsen" engraved in the blood tarnished blade. I gripped the sword tightly and smiled to myself as I slid down the cone. Now Dad would have to believe me.

The Middle Room

Billy stood outside the entrance gate and gazed up at the pink granite walls of his school. Butterflies fluttered in his tummy. Silhouetted by the early evening April sun, the building looked even more scary than usual. It had given him the creeps since the first day he started secondary school there, a year and a half ago now. The copper-topped belfry reminded him of the helmets worn by the Spanish conquistadors. He had recurring nightmares of a giant conquistador bursting out of the building and coming after him.

Despite the large windows, the school always seemed dark and gloomy inside. The middle room upstairs was the worst: no external windows, just glass panels along the corridor wall and a glass panel in the middle of the ceiling, covered in decades of damp and slime. Rumour had it that a ghost haunted the middle room; a ghost of a teacher who hung himself years ago. That room scared Billy the most, and was the reason he was here now. He swallowed the lump in his throat, walked through the gateway and headed around the back of the building, pondering the events that led up to this moment.

He had always been a target for bullies, due to him being shy and never standing up for himself. Events had worsened when a song called 'Billy Don't Be A Hero' reached number one in the pop charts a few weeks ago. Since then, some of the school kids had taunted him by singing adaptations of the song to humiliate him. The worst was Stanley Richards, who had gone out of his way to pick on Billy with rude and

19

hurtful versions of the song, especially when there were loads of other pupils about. Yesterday dinnertime, in the playground, Stanley had followed him around, shouting the song at the top of his voice. Eventually, Billy managed to run away and hide behind a bin around the back of the science block. It was there that Tony Blakely found him just as the bell went for lessons. Tony was the leader of the gang that Stanley was part of. Billy cringed when Tony appeared, expecting more taunting, or worse.

Tony walked up to him and said. 'Do you want to join my gang?'

This was the last thing Billy expected. 'What?'

'Look, if you join my gang and prove yourself, then Stanley and everyone else will leave you alone.'

'What do I have to do to prove myself?' Billy wiped away the snot running from his nose with the back of his hand

'Depends. What you scared of? Spiders? Heights? Tight spaces?

'Not really.'

'What then?'

'How do I know you won't tell everyone?'

'You don't, you just have to trust me.' With that Tony held out his hand.

'Why?'

'Because you seem like a nice guy, and I want to help you.'

Billy held out his hand so Tony could help him up, then realised it was the snot covered hand and quickly held out the other one. Tony grabbed the proffered hand and pulled Billy to his feet.

'Go on.' Billy said.

'Look, I could tell Stanley and everyone else to stop teasing you about that stupid song, but they'll just find some other reason to pick on you. If you do something to show your worth, then they'll leave you alone, permanently.'

'The middle room,' Billy blurted.

'What?'

'I'm afraid of the middle room.'

'In the school?'

'Yeah.'

'O...kay.' Tony paused for a few moments, a thoughtful look on his face. 'Be here tomorrow evening at six.'

'I will,' Billy replied, with dread.

Tony turned and started to walk away, then stopped. 'Why are you scared of that room?'

'Dunno, there's just something about it that gives me the creeps. Maybe it's the ghost of that teacher that hung himself.'

'Could be. See you tomorrow.'

As Billy rounded the corner to the playground at the back of the school, he saw the gang sprawled around, all twelve of them. Some were sitting or lying on the ground; others, including Tony and Stanley, were leaning against the rear wall of the school hall. Billy looked up to the windows on the floor above and felt an overwhelming urge to turn and run away. Beyond that room was the middle room. He stopped, and was about to turn, when Stanley spotted him.

'Here he is,' Stanley shouted, before breaking into song. 'Billy don't be a hero, don't be a fool–.'

Tony struck Stanley on the chest, driving the breath from him. 'Shut up, Stan.' He pushed away from the wall and walked towards Billy 'Glad you made it, Billy. You okay?'

'I guess.'

'You still wanna join my gang?'

Billy's gaze wandered over the staring faces of the gang members. Their expressions ranged from friendly to hostile, but most seemed friendly.

'Yeah, I still wanna join your gang.'

'Cool!' Tony said. 'You spend ten minutes in the middle room, alone, and you're in.'

Billy felt his bladder twitch and doubled over slightly, tensing. His hands involuntarily moving to his crotch.

'He's peed himself.' Stanley laughed.

'Billy?' Tony said, his expression serious.

Billy stood up straight, folded his arms across his chest and glared at Stanley.

'Okay. I'll do it.'

'Far out,' Tony said.

'How do we know he won't chicken out before he gets there?' Stanley said.

Tony grinned. 'Because you're going with him, Stan.'

'Sod off. Am I hell as like.'

'You're not scared, are you, Stanley? Scared of a ghosty-whosty? Billy's not scared, are you, Billy?'

'No,' Billy lied. 'But why him?'

'One, Stan has got one of those watches with a timer thingy. Two, he will watch you from the corridor and make sure you stay in there for ten minutes. Three, I know there's no chance of you two plotting together to cheat.'

'I'm in,' Stanley said, reluctantly.

'Okay,' Billy said, resigned to his fate. 'How do we get in?'

'I left this window on the catch during afternoon break.' Tony walked up to the back of the school hall and placed his fingers along the bottom edge of the large sash window. 'It looks locked but should open with a good shove.' With that, he braced himself and pushed the window up. 'Come on, Billy, I'll give you a leg up.'

He laced his fingers together and held them out in front, cupped. Billy stepped up and placed his right foot in the cup.

'When you get up there, come to the window above here, so we know you made it. Now, after three. One, two, three.'

Billy bounced on his left foot, building up momentum. On "three" he leapt up, grabbed the edge of the window ledge inside, pulled himself through and jumped down on to the parquet flooring of the hall. The sound of his landing echoing around the dim room. While he waited for Stanley, he gazed up at the ceiling at the other end of the hall. A shiver ran down his spine as he thought about the middle room above. The sound of Stanley's feet hitting the floor brought him back to himself.

'Ready then?' Stanley said.

'I guess.'

They headed out through the double doors at the other end of the hall and turned right along the corridor. Then up the concrete stairs that curved around until they reached the first-floor corridor. There they paused and looked at the glass panels along the outer edge of the middle room. The darkness seemed to ooze out through the glass. Billy slowly walked towards the room, a shaky hand reaching out for the door handle as he approached. He pushed open the door and peered into the gloom. As his eyes adjusted to the darkness, he made out the shapes of desks and chairs. The teacher's desk perched in the centre at the far side of the room. To the left of it, he could see the door that led into the room on the other side, the room that overlooked the playground. He felt, rather than heard, Stanley step up behind him.

'Better let the gang know we're here.'

Billy noted the tremor in Stanley's voice. He said nothing, but walked towards the other door, his eyes constantly scanning the middle room for anything untoward. Relief flooded through him as he opened the door and dim light entered the room. He rushed towards the left of the two windows that overlooked the playground, Stanley just behind him. The gang were all standing together and looking up at the windows. Stanley shoved past Billy and hammered on the window then gave a double thumbs up. Billy looked over Stanley's shoulder and noticed Tony nodding his head in approval.

Suddenly, the gang's view switched to the right-hand window and their faces fell in horror. Billy noticed Tony suddenly run towards the building. Stanley looked at the gang, puzzled. Billy turned towards the other window and felt his insides turn to jelly. There stood a ghostly figure of a man. He was short, wearing a three-piece tweed suit and a bow tie. A black gown hung from his shoulders. In his right hand, he held a bamboo cane. Billy reached up and grabbed

Stanley's shoulder, just as Stanley turned to face the figure, who was slowly raising the cane above his head.

'Get out of here!' Billy shouted, but Stanley was frozen to the spot. Billy's legs didn't seem to be responding as he wanted them to. He wanted them to run faster than they had ever run before, but the best they could manage was an uncoordinated lurch. He was halfway across the middle room when he heard a whooshing sound, and a crack. Stanley screamed. The sound chilled him to the bone and he stopped dead. Another whoosh, then crack. Stanley screamed again.

Without thinking about it, Billy turned and went back to help him.

Stanley staggered backwards, arms curled over his head, trying to ward of the impacts of the cane. Billy grabbed the back of Stanley's shirt with both hands and pulled him backwards, but not quickly enough to avoid Stanley receiving a glancing blow from the cane. Billy looked at the ghost's face and saw pure malevolence. The ghost raised the cane again and brought it down in a vicious, singing arc. Billy noticed the smell of urine coming from Stanley and yanked him into the middle room, so the cane missed its target. The ghost stepped backwards, paused, raised the cane and rushed forwards. This time the cane caught Stanley full on his forearm and he screamed again. Billy noticed the ghost step back again and pause as if expecting some form of retaliation. When none came, he raised the cane, struck again, then retreated a step. Just as realisation came to Billy, Tony ran in from the corridor.

Billy!' he cried.

Billy spun round and launched Stanley at Tony, just in time to avoid Stanley being hit again. 'Get him out of here,' he said.

He turned back to face the ghost, who had taken another step back and was raising the cane again. This time, Billy was the target.

As the cane reached the top of its arc Billy roared. 'NO!'

The ghost recoiled, as if struck by the power and authority

of Billy's voice. The ghost lowered the cane as it steadied itself. Billy pressed on towards the ghost, and it retreated another step. It seemed to fade a little.

'I know what you are,' Billy said with scorn as he continued to advance on the ghost. 'You're a bully and a coward, hiding behind a cane. Picking on defenceless schoolboys who can't fight back. When someone stands up to you, you run away. I bet that's why you hanged yourself, isn't it? I bet some schoolboy stood up to you in front of the others and they all laughed at you, didn't they?' The ghost faded some more. 'Oh, the shame you must have felt.' Billy laughed at the ghost as it faded almost to nothing. 'That's it, fade away you lily-livered coward, and don't come back again, ever.'

The ghost disappeared.

Billy turned to see Tony with his arms wrapped around a catatonic Stanley.

'Give us a hand Billy,' Tony said. 'Let's get out of here.'

Billy and Tony exited the building through a fire-door next to the hall, a slightly more responsive Stanley suspended between them. When they reached where the gang still stood, they lowered him down and leant his back against the hall wall.

'You okay, Stanley?' Tony said, checking the welts on Stanley's arms.

One of the gang members noticed the damp stain in the front of Stanley's trousers.

'He's pissed himself,' he said, and he started to laugh.

The rest of the gang joined in.

Billy leapt up and flew at the boy, grabbed his shirt and pulled him close until they were nose to nose. 'Leave him alone or I'll kick your bastard head in.' He released the boy with a shove and addressed the rest of the gang. 'If any one of you had been up there, you would have probably pissed AND shit yourself.'

Everyone stared at Billy in awe.

'Welcome to the gang, Billy,' Tony said. 'That's if you still want in.'

'Yeah, I'm in,' Billy said.

Too Hot and Too Bright

It's too hot and too bright, thought eight-year-old Alice as she walked along Marlborough Road towards her grandparents' house. The first week of the summer holidays and she was already bored. She thought about going to the Bowling Green playground to see if there were other girls there to play with, but decided against. She was too shy, and scared that the other girls might make fun of her.

Too hot and too bright. Her yellow cotton dress clung to her sweaty back and made her itch. The heat from the pavement burnt her feet through the soles of her red leather sandals. The smell of melting tarmac filled the air. The man on the telly said this was the hottest summer since records began. Alice couldn't work out the connection between hot summers and record players, but agreed that summer 1976 was hot.

Too hot and too bright. The sun reflecting off the walls of the terraced houses made her squint. As Alice passed a newly painted house, the glare from the white was so bright it hurt her eyes. She raised both hands to shade them. The sweat on her forehead wet her fingers.

Too hot and too bright. Too still and too quiet, as well. Apart from Alice, nothing moved; no people, no cars, no birds, not even one of the billions of Ladybirds that the man on the telly said had invaded Britain. At the far end of the street, she could see a small patch of blue water in the harbour, framed by the road, the houses either side, and the strip of the Roseland Peninsula visible beyond. Even the water was still; not a boat or breeze-blown ripple disturbed the surface.

No sounds either. No hammering from the Docks, no bumble bees humming by as they made their erratic flights in search of flowers. Not even the screech and yell of a seagull. This silence was a rare event in Falmouth.

Too hot and too bright and too still and t... wait. What was that?

She stopped and stared at a disturbance in the air a little way ahead of her. A strange shimmering above the pavement. She tried to make out what it was. It was different to heat haze; it had a faint outline and moved about randomly. Alice bit her bottom lip, wondering what to do. She was about to cross the road to avoid whatever it was, when it suddenly separated into three parts, each of which rushed towards her.

She shrieked and turned to run but the three shapes surrounded her. She stood there, eyes wide and mouth agape, while the three shapes bobbed up and down and circled around her. A scream built within her, but before she had chance to release it, the three shapes moved away. They went along the pavement for a short distance then headed across the road towards the side street down to Florence Terrace.

Alice watched their progress, unsure what to do. Part of her wanted to run to the safety of Grandma's house, but another, smaller part, wanted to know more about the shimmering shapes. As they passed out of view, Alice made her decision. She stopped briefly at the kerb to do a quick Green Cross Code, then hurried across the road. By the time she reached the side street, two of the shapes had disappeared from sight but the third was still visible. Just as it turned the corner into a back lane, part of it passed through shade.

Alice stopped dead in her tracks. A cold shiver ran down her hot back. Was that an arm and hand?

Her mind reeled in fear and indecision. Then one of Grandma's wise old sayings came to her: "Curiosity killed the cat, but satisfaction brought it back." Sweat dripped from her face as she ran towards the back lane.

She stopped at the entrance and looked along the lane. One side was in the shadow cast by the high wall that ran along the rear of the houses. The other side was bright with sunshine.

There. In a gateway on the shaded side, Alice could see the faint outline of a blue hoop-bottomed dress sticking out beyond the gateway. It looked like the dresses children wore in Victorian times. She remembered them from school history lessons.

Alice crept warily along the sunny side of the lane, keeping her distance in case whoever was hiding in the gateway meant her harm. As she drew level with the gateway, the wearer of the dress came into view. A little girl. Younger than Alice. As well as the hooped-dress, the girl wore a bonnet, tied on with a ribbon. Alice was taken aback when she realised she could see through the girl to the gate behind.

A ghost?

The hairs rose on the back of her neck. The girl looked straight at Alice, smiling, happy to be found.

Was this a game of hide and seek?

The girl stepped from the gateway, towards Alice, a finger to her lips for secrecy. With her other hand, she discretely pointed to the next gateway along the lane. Alice walked towards her; she shivered as she moved into the cool shade. Alice pointed to the next gateway and mimed tiptoeing to it. The little girl covered her mouth as if to stifle a giggle, but Alice heard no sound. They set off together, keeping close to the wall, until they reached the open gateway. The little girl pointed at the wall to the right of the gateway to show there was someone on the other side. Alice nodded, then held up three fingers, counted them off, then mimed jumping through the gateway. The little girl stifled another silent giggle. Alice counted to three and they leapt through the gateway. Another girl was hiding behind the wall. She jumped in fright as Alice and the little girl suddenly appeared. The little girl laughed, silently. The new girl wore the same type of Victorian dress and bonnet, but was closer to Alice's height and age. She was also semi-transparent, but Alice wasn't worried by that anymore.

'Found you,' Alice said.

The girl held up her hands in mock surrender. Alice pointed towards the little girl.

'Is this your sister?'

She nodded.

The little girl moved beside her sister, pointed at her, then said something to Alice.

'I'm sorry I can't hear what you are saying.'

The little girl gave Alice a thoughtful look. It seemed that she could hear Alice speak fine. The girl looked around the garden. She ran to a rosebush, pointed at one of the flowers then pointed to her sister.

'Rose? Your sister is called Rose?'

The little girl noiselessly clapped her hands with joy.

'My name is Alice.'

The little girl's eyes widened and she stared at Alice in awe. Then jumped up and down, pointing at herself.

'You're called Alice too?'

The little girl nodded vigorously.

'Well, I'm very pleased to meet you Alice, and you too Rose.'

Rose gave a small curtsey.

'Weren't there three of you?

The sisters nodded.

'What's the other one's name?'

Rose pondered for a moment then held out both hands in front of her, a few inches apart. She raised them up, as if she was putting something on her head, and then pointed her fingers upwards.

'A crown? Like a Queen? Is it Victoria?'

Rose and little Alice burst into silent laughter.

'Not a Queen then.'

As the sisters continued their soundless amusement, Alice

thought back to her history lessons. What was Queen Victoria's husband called?

'Albert!'

Rose smiled and nodded.

'How old is he?'

Little Alice raised both hands, all ten digits outstretched. She held them up for a second, then closed all but two fingers into fists.

'Twelve?'

Little Alice smiled and clapped her muted hands with joy.

'Where is he? Is he hiding?'

Rose nodded and pointed to the gateway, then held out a hand for her little sister to hold. With her other hand she gestured for Alice to go first, and the three of them went back out to the lane.

Alice looked up and down the lane but couldn't see anyone. She turned to Rose and little Alice. They were both scanning the lane for Albert.

'Can you see him?' Alice said.

Both sisters shook their heads. Alice continued her search, scouring amongst the branches of a tree that overhung a wall further along the lane. The tree was on the opposite side of the lane, the sunny side. So instead of looking for a boy, Alice looked for a shimmering.

It took a few moments but eventually she saw it; along the top of the wall, just beyond the tree. She turned to the sisters and quietly told them where Albert was. The both looked in that direction, then Little Alice ran towards the wall, fading to a shimmer as she crossed the lane. She stood beneath the wall for a few seconds then stepped back as Albert jumped down from the wall. The two of them crossed the lane back into shadow. Little Alice was talking animatedly to Albert whilst gesturing towards her namesake. As they approached Alice noticed Albert was taller than she was. He wore a peaked cap, a blazer, and short trousers. He stopped in front of Alice, smiled at her then bowed. Alice curtsied and smiled back. What a handsome chap he was.

'Pleased to meet you Albert. That was a good hiding place, up on the wall.'

He shook his head, pointed at Alice then pointed to his eye and finally to his chest.

'I almost missed seeing you, hidden behind that tree.'

Suddenly, the three siblings were alerted by something behind Alice. She turned to look but couldn't see anything. She turned to Rose and gave her a questioning look.

'What is it?'

Rose raised her hands to either side of her mouth and pretended to call out.

'Someone is calling you?'

Rose nodded.

'Do you have to go now?'

Another nod.

'Awww, that's a shame. I was having so much fun.'

Albert, Rose and Little Alice all nodded in unison.

'Well thank you for letting me play hide and seek with you. I hope we get to play again sometime.'

Albert bowed, Rose and Alice curtsied.

Alice curtsied back then stepped aside.

Albert took a sister's hand in each of his and the three of them headed along the lane. When they reached the gate where Little Alice had hidden earlier, the three children separated, turned and waved. Alice waved back, then the three children went through the gateway.

Alice smiled to herself, turned away and skipped down the lane towards Grandma's house, crossing back into the heat of the sunshine as she went. Maybe she would go to the Bowling Green playground on the way, see if there anyone there to play with.

It was still too hot, too hot and too bright, but that was okay.

Cliffhanger

It was the second week of the summer holidays when Chris and his best friend Matt headed, side by side, up the path from Gyllyngvase Beach towards Swanpool Beach. The early afternoon sunlight seemed too bright on Chris's eyes, the heat uncomfortable on his exposed face and arms. The beach was packed with people enjoying the sea and sand. Hundreds of individual voices built to a sudden tumult when the intermittent breeze from the sea carried the sound towards them; a breeze that also carried the tang of salt and seaweed. As the path levelled and narrowed, they walked in single file, Matt taking the lead. Chris's attention was drawn to a speedboat skimming along the waves out in the bay. He raised his hand to shade his eyes from the sun and squinted to reduce the glare of the diamond reflections from the sea. He was just about to comment on the boat, when he heard Matt quietly murmur:

'Woah. See that girl there. What a stunner.'

Chris looked ahead. Further along the path, a girl leaned on the wooden fencing, looking out to sea. Long brown hair cascaded over a blue summer dress. Slender legs led down to tiny feet in leather sandals. The girl suddenly turned towards them. A smile broke on her face and she waved.

Chris was dumbstruck. The girl was beautiful, and not in a small way. For the best part of his sixteen years, girls had been something he generally ignored, unless they were being really annoying. Recently, however, girls of his age had become very interesting. They smelt nice and had figures with curves that Chris found intriguing. Their hands and fingers seemed very delicate and looked like they might be nice to hold, if ever the chance arose.

'Hi, I'm Rachel,' she said.

'Hi. I'm Matt, and this is Chris.'

'Err...yeah...I'm Chris.' His brain struggled to cope with the combination of talking, walking, and a girl saying hello. The girl looked familiar, but he couldn't think where he'd seen her before.

'You from around here?' Matt asked.

'Just visiting.'

'Where do you live? How old are you?' Chris blurted, his stomach turning somersaults.

He noticed a look of pain flicker across Rachel's face momentarily, a slight tension around her brown, almond-shaped eyes.

'Don't be so nosey, Chris.' Matt turned and gave him a glaring look that roughly translated as: "Don't be such a dumbass. That's a girl talking to us."

'Sorry, I was only trying to be friendly.'

'It's okay,' Rachel said, the smile returning to her face. 'You guys up to much?'

'Nah, just out for a walk,' Matt said. 'We wanted to go swimming this afternoon but Chris's got to go visit some rellies with his Mum and Dad in a bit.'

'Yeah, Auntie Joan and Uncle Mike are down on holiday in their caravan,' Chris said. 'So it will be an afternoon of endless, pointless questions and their annoying yappy dog humping my leg. Major Dullsville.'

Rachel chuckled at his description.

Chris blushed; a girl had laughed at his joke. His heart pounded in his chest. He swallowed, trying to wet his suddenly dry mouth.

Matt noticed his discomfort and butted in. 'You free any other time, Rachel?'

'This evening,' she replied, a sudden urgency in her voice. 'Here, at six 'o clock?'

'Sounds good,' Matt said. 'Will you be back by then,

Chris?'

'Should be, if that annoying dog hasn't worn my leg away.'

Rachel chuckled again. 'My best friend, Alison, will be here. You'll like her. She's funny, like you.'

At that moment, Chris wished his Auntie, Uncle and annoying dog were far, far away so he could meet Alison right now.

'Can't wait to meet her,' he replied.

'Six it is then,' Matt said.

'It's a date,' Rachel said.

The boys continued along the footpath. Chris was in a daze. He had a date with a girl. Maybe, a potential girlfriend. As the boys turned to walk up some steps he glanced back towards Rachel. She was staring at the floor, hands clasped together in front of her. She seemed to notice their gaze and quickly looked up. She smiled and gave another wave before turning and walking away.

At five to six, the boys headed along the path again. Chris regaled Matt with the details of the visit to Auntie Joan. Matt laughed at the tale of woe.

'...And all the time she's interrogating me, the sodding dog was trying to shag my leg off,' Chris said, before continuing in his best Auntie Joan screechy voice, '"He only does it 'cos he likes you," and I'm thinking why doesn't he go and like a bramble bush. I swear I'll...'

Matt elbowed him gently and said, 'Look, that must be Alison.'

Chris gazed at the girl leaning on the fencing exactly as Rachel had earlier. Alison had black, shoulder-length, wavy hair, and was wearing a red T-shirt and blue jeans. She looked sad as she gazed down at the rocks below. Chris's heart ached. It seemed so wrong that such a pretty girl could look so sad.

'Hi,' Matt said.

The girl, startled, stood up straight and looked at the boys warily.

'I'm Matt, and this is Chris. You must be Alison.'

'I don't know you,' she said with suspicion.

'Rachel said to meet you both here at six,' Matt said.

At Matt's words, Alison's whole manner turned frosty. 'Really? When did she say this?'

'This afternoon.' Matt said.

'You sick fuck! Did Mickey Downey put you up to this?' Alison demanded. 'If so it's a pretty nasty joke.'

'I'm not joking. We were right here, talking to her, weren't we, Chris.'

'Where is she?' Chris asked, shocked by Alison's outburst. 'Isn't she coming?'

'Well that's pretty unlikely, isn't it?'

Chris and Matt looked at each other, confused.

Alison stared at them. 'You really don't know, do you?'

'Know what?' Matt asked.

'She's dead,' Alison said. 'Rachel is dead.'

Matt and Chris stared at Alison, stunned.

'But...but…we…' Chris's mind whirled.

'How? When?' Matt asked.

'A year ago today. On the rocks below here.' Alison turned, leaned on the railing and looked down to the beach below.

'She fell?' Matt peered down to the rock.

Alison snorted contemptuously. 'That's the official story. See this top railing that's newer than the others? Well, allegedly, she was leaning on the old rotten one that was here, when it collapsed, and she fell head-first down there. Personally, I think she was murdered.'

Chris noted how the railing looked newer than the adjacent rails.

'Murdered?' Matt sounded doubtful. 'Who by?'

'Mickey Downey,' Chris said, recovering his senses at last. That was why Rachel looked familiar. He'd seen a photo of her in the local paper last year, after she died. He recalled rumours that a local Hell's Angel called Mickey Downey was somehow involved with it, but nothing had come of the suspicion.

You know him?' Alison asked.

'Know of him,' Chris replied. 'He's the leader of the that local biker gang, isn't he? The Moped Mob.'

Alison laughed and Chris blushed.

'That's the ones. Always cruising around town, trying to look cool on their 50cc bikes.'

'I think I know who you mean,' Matt said. 'About ten of them in the gang, most of them about our age. The leader's a bit older, rides a proper motorbike. Always wears a denim cut-off jacket, got a big shark-tooth pendant.'

'Probably piss himself if he ever met a shark,' Chris said.

Alison burst out laughing. 'You're right there. That's Mickey Downey. Rachel was going out with him. I always told her she was mad going out with a loser like that, but she loved riding on the back of his motorbike. Had a bit of a wild rebellious streak, did Rachel. Anyway, Rachel was fifteen when she went out with him. He was eighteen. She didn't mind snogging him, but eventually he started wanting more than Rachel was prepared to give, if you know what I mean.'

Chris contemplated Alison's words then blushed.

Alison noticed his discomfort and laughed. 'You are funny. Cute, but funny.' Her smile faded. 'When Rachel refused to let him have his way, he started getting nasty. She put up with it for a while, but when he started calling her a "frigid bitch" and showing her up in front of his gang, she decided to end it. She arranged to meet him down at Gylly beach to tell him it was over. Next thing is, she's dead on the beach below.

'Didn't the police arrest him?' Matt asked.

Alison turned to look out into the bay. 'They did, but his mates covered for him. Said he was with them. Nobody else witnessed seeing him being around here, and there was no evidence to place him here, so the police let him go. Said it was a tragic accident.'

'But you don't believe that,' Matt said.

'I know it was him. I've seen him a few times since, and he won't look me in the face. Guilt written all over him.'

Matt and Chris moved forward and leant on the railing next to Alison. The three of them gazed into the distance, thinking.

After a minute or two, Matt said, 'So why was Rachel here earlier?'

Alison turned and stared right into Matt's face. 'Are you saying for real that you saw her? That you spoke with her?'

Matt nodded. 'As real as I'm talking to you, right now.'

She looked at Chris, who nodded.

Alison's eyes filled with tears. 'Great,' she said, throwing back her head, 'thanks Rachel. I spend a year breaking my heart, talking to you, missing you, and you show up for two total strangers.'

Chris didn't know what to do or say. He wanted to comfort her, but a crying girl was out of his comfort zone, so he just stared down at the beach.

'Here!' came Rachel's voice from below and slightly to the left. All three looked in that direction.

'Rachel?' Alison said.

'You heard it too?' Matt said. 'Did you hear it, Chris?'

'Yeah.' Chris pointed to a spot about ten feet down. 'Came from down there.'

'There's something in that bush,' Matt said.

Chris angled his head and stared harder. 'Yeah, I see it.'

'Oh God.' Alison clasped a hand to her face. 'I think I know what it is. Can you get it?'

'Reckon so.' Chris climbed over the fence and scurried down the steep bank, holding onto the plants growing out of it, to slow his descent. When he reached the object, he spent a few seconds freeing it from the bush before turning and looking up to Alison.

'Catch.' He threw the object up and she caught it in both hands.

Chris clambered back up the bank, and with Matt's help on the last bit, the three of them were stood together on the path again.

'Well, at least we now know why Rachel showed up for you and not me. I would never have been able to climb down there. Thank you both.'

'So what was it you found?' Matt asked.

Alison held open her hand and showed him.

'A shark-tooth pendant on a leather thong,' Chris said.

'Probably torn from Mickey Downey's neck by Rachel when he pushed her over the edge.'

'So that's proof he killed her.' Matt said. 'We can go to the police and have him arrested.'

'I doubt it.' Alison ran her thumb over the enamel of the tooth. 'The police will probably say it could have been dropped there at anytime, by anybody.'

'So, me going down there after it was a waste of time?'

Alison looked out to sea and pondered for a few moments. 'Not necessarily.'

'What are you thinking?' Matt asked.

Alison tapped the tooth with her nail. 'I'm thinking I might give it back to him.'

'What?' Chris shook his head. 'You can't mean that?'

'I know it sounds crazy, but I have this strong feeling that Rachel wants me to give it back to Mickey Downey.' Alison clenched the necklace tight in her fist. 'Yes, I'm sure that's what she wants.' She looked at both of them and grinned. 'So that's what I'm going to do.'

Mickey Downey and his gang were parked up at the bus stop by the Prince of Wales Pier when Alison crossed the road towards them. Matt and Chris watched from up the hill, on the corner of Webber Street. Chris had wanted the three of them to confront Mickey Downey, but Alison insisted that she should do it alone.

'Hey Mickey,' Alison said. 'Catch this, your asshole.'

She threw the shark's tooth pendant at him. He caught it instinctively, looked at it, then stared at Alison, blue eyes wide with shock.

'Guess where I found it?' she said accusingly. 'Or should I say, guess where you lost it?'

Mickey said nothing, but the look on his tanned, chiselled face spoke volumes.

'Don't worry, your secret is safe with me...and Rachel.' With that, Alison turned and walked away.

Mickey laughed as she departed. 'Stupid bitch,' he shouted after her, but she ignored him.

His gang laughed at the insult and then watched as he hung the shark-tooth pendant around his neck. It felt a bit tighter than he remembered, probably the leather had shrunk, but it felt good to be wearing it again.

'Come on losers,' he said to his gang. 'Let's get out of here.'

'Well, that's the end of that,' Alison said, as she returned to where Matt and Chris waited for her.

'I can't believe you're going to let him get away with murder,' Matt said.

'There's nothing more I can do,' she replied.

'You busy next Saturday, Alison?' Chris murmured, staring at the ground and shuffling his feet nervously.

'Are you asking me out, Chris?' Alison smirked.

Matt looked at Chris in awe.

'Well...kind of...I s'pose...' Chris said.

'Then, yes, definitely.' She threw her arms around Chris's neck and kissed him on the cheek.

Chris blushed furiously, gently wrapping his arms around her waist. An overwhelming feeling of joy flooded through him; he had a girl in his arms. No, he had a girlfriend in his arms. He never wanted the moment to end, but eventually Alison released him and stepped out of his embrace.

She smiled then chuckled. 'Come on, guys, let's go in the café there and celebrate with Coke and ice cream. I'm buying.'

Later that evening, after his biker gang had dispersed for the night, Mickey Downey was bombing down Dracaena Avenue at sixty miles per hour on his bike when he felt the leather of the pendant tighten around his throat. He jammed on the brakes and nearly lost control of the bike. He pulled over, removed his helmet and tried to get his fingers under the leather thong, but as soon as he touched it, it tightened more, cutting into his neck. He reached around the back of his neck with both hands and tried to undo the clasp, but it was seized solid. He was struggling for breath when he heard a voice behind him.

'Hello Mickey,' Rachel said. 'Glad to have your pendant back?'

He spun round, light-headed, and nearly fell over.

'Rachel?' Mickey gasped. 'But you're dead.'

'And so will you be, soon,' Rachel said.

'Fuck you, Rachel,' Mickey growled. 'Fuck you to hell and ba...'

The thong tightened again, cutting off his airways. Lights flashed in his head and he slipped into unconsciousness and collapsed to the ground.

'Oh no, Mickey.' Rachel leaned over and whispered in his ear. 'I'm not the one going to hell. You are.'

The Tunnel

Aaron lay awake in his bed. He could hear Mum and Dad arguing downstairs in the bar again. It seemed to happen a lot these days. He pulled the covers up over his head to block out the noise but he could still hear their muffled voices. Things hadn't been going well recently. Mum and Dad had bought the Sportsman's Arms a few years before, and to start with, things had been good. Dad loved running the pub and Mum had started doing bar meals, which had been a big hit with the locals. There were plans to change the beer cellar into toilets. At present, the toilets were outside in the back yard, which meant going out the front door of the pub, up the hill, and in through the back gate. The toilets were cold and home to scary spiders. Indoor toilets would be a major improvement.

Recently, things had changed. The news was always going on about how there was a world-wide oil crisis, and how everyone in Britain was on strike all the time. A lot of the time, there was no electric, so the beer pumps didn't work and the pub had to be lit by candles. The final straw had been a lack of fish in the sea for the local fisherman to catch. The fishermen were the bulk of the pub's customers, and without them, the money dried up. Dad originally employed a builder to convert the cellar, but now he was having to do it all himself. The rows had started about that time, always about money. Mum was worried about unpaid bills and the overdraft getting bigger. Dad was convinced things would get better soon.

Aaron wasn't sure if he had dozed off under the covers,

but he could no longer hear Mum and Dad arguing. He threw back the covers and nearly screamed. Stood at the foot of the bed was the figure of a man. Old, with a wispy grey beard and dark robes. He looked like a monk.

'My name is Dominic,' the man said. 'and I would ask a favour of you.'

Aaron yanked the covers back up to his chin. 'Favour?' he said, and it came out as a squeak.

The man nodded and made to move closer, but when Aaron squealed and backed up the bed until his shoulders were pressed against the headboard, the sheet still held tight against him, the man stopped where he was, then took a step back.

'Fear not,' he said. 'I mean you no harm. I want only to talk with you of something that might help you, and your family.' He waited until Aaron lowered the sheet a fraction and nodded for him to go on. 'Near to this place is a well near the shoreline, do you know of what I speak?'

'Well Beach, yeah. It's just down the hill.'

'There is a tunnel that runs from there to this place. A smuggler's passage. Do you know of it?'

A smuggler's passage? Aaron knew about Cornish smugglers and their tunnels, but he'd never heard of one around Falmouth. Was the man saying there used to be one right here, at their own pub?

'I don't know about any tunnel,' he said. 'But I don't think there've been any smugglers round here for a long time.'

A sad look passed across Dominic's face. I pray it still exists,' he said, 'for hidden within the passage, is a casket.'

'What sort of casket?' Aaron asked, more curious now than scared.

'Would you be prepared to search for it?'

'Will it be dangerous?'

Dominic looked Aaron straight in the eye and with a serious tone said. 'There may be perils, but I believe you will prevail, as all heroes must.'

Aaron gazed at the Dr Who poster on the wall and thought about Dominic's request. Dr Who was Aaron's hero, so clever and brave. This could be an adventure like Dr Who had. He had a mission to accomplish.

'What's in the casket?'

'The casket contains documents and various artefacts. The documents were hidden because the time was not right to reveal their contents, but enough time has passed that it would now be safe for them to become public knowledge.'

'Just documents? No treasure?'

The man smiled. 'There will be all the treasure you need.'

'What if I can't find the tunnel?'

'Then the documents will remain secret, and the information, and the treasure, will be lost forever.'

Aaron stared at the man, who no longer looked frightening, just worried.

'Well, I'll try,' he said, 'but I can't promise anything.'

'I can ask no more than that. The casket is hidden within a hollow near the top of the tunnel. Good luck, and good fortune to you.'

Aaron shut his eyes and pictured Mum and Dad's faces when he came home with a box of treasure. When he opened them again, Dominic had vanished.

Aaron fell asleep dreaming of smugglers and treasure and tunnels and heroes, and a Mum and Dad who no longer argued.

The next morning, Aaron was down on Well Beach straight after breakfast. He didn't tell his parents where he was going. Mum was busy cleaning the bar and Dad was getting ready to do some work in the beer cellar. Aaron knew about the well at the top of the beach, but could see nothing on the cliffs and banks to denote a tunnel or passage. That only left the cellars. The cellars were two rooms built high into the cliff face and fronted with a wall made from large square-cut granite blocks. The only way into the cellars was through two narrow slits in the wall.

Aaron didn't like going in there. The cellars were unnaturally cold, and smelt old and bad. Plucking up courage, he scrambled up the wall and into the left-hand cellar. The cold hit him like a wave and the darkness descended like a blanket. Shivering, he pulled out the small torch from his pocket and switched it on. The beam struggled to penetrate the darkness. He could just make out the compacted soil floor and the rough stone walls of the cellar, but the ceiling was too high to be seen. The smell of rot and damp made his nose twitch and his stomach churn.

Covering his mouth with his free hand, he began examining the walls for a tunnel entrance. Reason told him that the entrance couldn't be too high up if it was once a smuggler's tunnel. Once he was sure there was no tunnel in the first cellar, he went through the opening that led the few feet in to the other cellar.

He searched around but still found no tunnel. The cold caused him to shake. He moved to the entrance slit and tried to warm himself in the morning sun. While he stood there, gazing out across the harbour, he pondered the problem. There was no sign of the tunnel on the cliffs outside, and none in the chambers. Where else was there?

The answer came to him suddenly; the opening between the cellars.

He moved back to the arched opening and shone his torch at it. There, at the rear side, was a large vertical slab of what appeared to be slate. It was about three feet high and two feet wide and set flush with the stones around it. He tried getting his fingers in the gap around the edge but couldn't get a grip on it. He needed something to lever with. Something thin, but strong. The coal bunker shovel in the back yard of the pub would do. He ran home and got it, sneaking in so mum or dad wouldn't see and ask questions.

Aaron made his way back to the slit, threw the shovel in then climbed back up into the cellar. He held the torch in his mouth and used the metal bar to prise the slate slab away from the wall. He had to jump out of the way as the slab fell over and hit the ground with a thud.

He took the torch out of his mouth, crouched down and shone the beam in through the hole. A few feet in on the other side, he could see some steps hewn into the rock. Getting down on his hands and knees, he crawled through the hole.

Immediately on the other side, the tunnel opened up wide enough and high enough for Aaron to stand up. He carefully made his way up the steps and on to a path that veered up and off to the left. The torch beam lit up the rough walls of the tunnel. It must have taken ages to hack a way through. The path was quite steep and the sound of his feet on the rock echoed up and down the tunnel. The exertion of the climb made him breathless, so he stopped to rest. As he rested, he shone his torch around the tunnel. The light sparkled on the mica in the yellow granite.

Aaron heard a noise. It sounded like someone breathing behind him.

He turned and shone the torch back down the tunnel. Was someone, or something, creeping up on him? He held his breath as he searched the tunnel. The sound stopped suddenly. It was then that Aaron realised the sound was his own breathing echoing around. He laughed at himself. Idiot.

Reassured, he continued up the path. At one point, the roof of the tunnel had collapsed and partially blocked the way. He had to scramble over the debris on his hands and knees, ducking his head to squeeze through the gap. Once clear, he wondered how much longer the tunnel was. It seemed like he had been walking for ages. He stopped again. He could hear a hammering sound. The sound reverberated through the tunnel, so he couldn't make out if it was ahead or behind him.

His imagination ran riot. Was there a ghost or monster in the tunnel waiting for him? Had Dominic tricked him and set him up to be captured?

His torch's beam was getting dimmer. Should he continue or turn and flee? He decided to go a bit further. If he didn't find the place where the casket was hidden soon, he would give up and turn back.

As he proceeded onwards, the hammering grew louder. He was about to give up when he noticed a triangular gap in the wall of the tunnel. It was a couple of feet wide at the bottom then tapered to nothing at about head height. It looked like a natural fissure as opposed to something man made. Aaron knelt down and crawled through the opening. The fading light of the torch showed that it went back about six feet. On the floor at the end, he could make out the shape of a box.

The casket.

He wriggled into the tight space until he could reach out and pull the casket towards him. Then he crawled backwards dragging it with him.

Once back in the tunnel, he examined the box. It was about a foot long and six inches high and wide. Made from a wood that was so dark it was almost impossible to see the grain running through it. Aaron could just make out a slight indentation along the edges where the lid met the bottom. A sturdy iron hinge ran along the back of the box, and a metal-rimmed keyhole marked the front. It was beautifully made. It was also locked.

The hammering brought him back to his situation. The torch was getting dimmer and he needed to get back outside. He lifted the box and was grateful that it wasn't too heavy. Just as he was about to head back, he heard a loud crack from down the tunnel, followed by a deafening crash. A cloud of dust rushed towards Aaron. He turned and ran up the tunnel but the cloud of dust overtook him, stinging his eyes and blinding him. He choked on the dust as he ran. The roof of the tunnel got lower and lower, until he was bent over, the box banging on his knees with every step. He tripped and fell. The box and torch flew from his grasp. The torch hit the ground and went out. Its final illumination was of a dead-end to the tunnel, before everything went black. Aaron lay on the ground, his head resting on his arms, and gasped for breath in the dust-filled tunnel.

The hammering stopped.

The sudden silence filled him with terror. Was something coming for him in the darkness? Sneaking up on him? Was he going to die here, killed by some unknown monster? Or would he be trapped here forever, buried alive until he starved to death? He hadn't told anyone where he was going, so no-one would come looking. Tears filled his eyes and despair overwhelmed him.

As he lay there sobbing, his thoughts were interrupted by a loud metallic creaking sound coming from above. A thin shaft of light appeared and shone down through the dust-filled air. A second creaking sound, and the shaft of light grew wider. Aaron lifted his head and gazed up into the light. Above his head, a rectangular hole had opened up. Another creak. The hole got bigger. Aaron could see two legs and the end of a crowbar at the edge of the hole. He then heard someone cough as the dust rose out of the hole.

'Dad?' Aaron said.

A face appeared, framed by the hole.

'Aaron? What the h... what on earth are you doing down there?' Dad said.

Aaron reached up with both arms and felt the firm grip of hands as Dad pulled him out of the hole. As soon as he was clear and his feet were on the floor, Aaron leapt up, wrapped his arms around Dad and held on to him for all he was worth.

Dad hugged him back. 'You could have been killed, Son.' He lowered him down. 'Come on, let's get you cleaned up, then you can tell me how the heck you ended up under the beer cellar floor.'

'The box. Dad there's a box down there. It's important.'

Dad knelt down at the edge of the hole and reached down into it. He felt around until he found the box then grabbed it and pulled it out.

'Right, come on, Aaron, upstairs, now.'

Three days later, Aaron and Dad walked into empty the pub where Mum was tidying up behind the bar.

She smiled when she saw them. 'How'd it go?'

'Great,' Dad said.

'The man at Truro Museum said the documents in the box were of important historical significance,' Aaron said. 'He said the gold coins are worth a fortune,'

'Of which we will hopefully receive a share,' Dad said. 'The find needs to be reported to the local coroner who will investigate. It's likely our reward will be enough to solve all our financial problems, anyway.'

Mum smiled at Aaron. 'My little hero saves the day.'

It was the biggest, brightest smile Aaron had seen on her face in months. Mission accomplished.

The Beacon Ghost

I have never believed in ghosts. As a child, I gave myself nightmares when I read ghost stories before bedtime or watched Hammer House of Horror movies on the television. But, because I never encountered a ghost, I reasoned they weren't real. When I grew up, the supernatural didn't figure in my world view at all: life was busy enough with the general day to day to think about such fancies.

A few days ago, I left my home in Claremont Cottages to visit some friends over at Old Hill. It was early evening as I headed up the lane, through the gap in the hedge and on to the Beacon. The sun had started to set, washing the drawing night with a red hue. A blackbird sang its evening chorus, perched on the branch of an ash tree. The smell of fresh cut grass mingled with the salty tang of the sea air.

The Beacon is famously named because it was the first in a line of fire beacons, lit between Falmouth and London, to relay the news of Nelson's victory at the Battle of Trafalgar. Less famous is the fact that years later it became a rubbish tip. The tip was where the refuse from the Falmouth area was collected, before being burned to generate electricity in the power station next to it. When people realised that the smoke from burnt rubbish was not good for the environment, or the local people, it was shut down, and the rubbish tip covered with earth and grassed over to make a public space.

All that remains of the tip nowadays is an incongruous twenty-foot high pipe that sticks out of the ground to vent the combustible fumes from the decomposed rubbish. A green-painted and rust-aged ionic style base supports an eight-inch diameter pipe that reaches for the sky. It is said that on certain nights, if you stand near the pipe, you can hear the moans of someone who was buried alive at the tip when a huge pile of rubbish collapsed on them. Nonsense. The moans are just the wind, or more particularly the north-east wind, as it blows across the open top of the pipe.

Then on Wednesday last, I walked up the Beacon and saw a young boy stood in the middle of the field. I didn't pay much mind to him; just a boy out walking his dog or something. I continued on my way. I spent a pleasant evening with my friends and headed back home around eleven o' clock. I was very perturbed to see the boy was still there. To see someone of such a tender age out at that late hour was cause for concern, so I decided to investigate. As I approached him, I noticed that his clothes were unusual: old fashioned - black ankle boots, black knee-length stockings, brown breeches and a white collarless shirt. The sort of thing my grandfather might have worn at that age. The boy seemed lost. He looked around, trying to find something.

I stopped a few yards from him. I didn't want to startle him, so I softly said, 'Are you all right?'

He didn't appear to notice me - just kept on looking around.

I tried again, a bit louder. 'Hello? Can you hear me?'

He turned and looked at me. His expression flickered between confusion and desperation.

'I can't find me Mum,' he said.

I crouched down so I looked straight at him, and tried to appear calm and relaxed, but inside I felt anxious. Something was very wrong with this situation. Questions rushed through my mind, but I pushed most of them aside.

'What's your name?'

'Thomas Lander.'

'Where do you live, Thomas?'

'Claremont Cottages.'

I frowned. I had lived at Claremont Cottages for many years. I knew all my neighbours, past and present. None of them were called Lander. The anxious feeling I'd had when I first spoke to him returned. I calmed myself and continued.

'What happened to you?'

'I was playing on the rubbish tip, looking for old toys and stuff. As I climbed one of the mounds of rubbish, it started to move-'

'Wait, the rubbish tip?' I looked all around us at the field of grass, whose history this boy was surely too young to know.

The boy nodded. 'All the rubbish slid down. I fell over and got carried along with it. Next thing I know, I'm here, but I don't know where here is. I called for me Mum over and over but she mustn't have heard, 'cause she never came.' He stopped speaking and wiped his nose on his sleeve.

I stared at him. He was standing right there, before my very eyes. Not believing he existed wasn't an option. I could have wept at his words. If he was who I now knew he must be, he would have been looking for his mother for decades.

'It's all right, Thomas,' I said, having no idea how I might make that true. 'I'll help you.'

'Do you know what year it is, Thomas?'

'Umm. No.'

'No matter. Do you know who is king?'

'King George the Fifth.'

I tried to recall my history lessons from school. George the Fifth was king during the first world-war, and reigned for twenty-odd years. Any last remnants of doubt I might have been harbouring were swept away.

'Do you remember the war, Thomas?'

'I was born at the beginning of the war. Me Dad went off to fight and never came back.'

My thoughts immediately went to Thomas' mother. She had lost a husband and a child in the course of a few years.

'How old are you, Thomas?'

'Eight and a half.'

I did some mental calculations. Thomas was probably born in 1915 and died around 1923-24. His mum was likely born in the last decade of the 19th century. So the chances of her still being alive were pretty slim.

'Mister? Will you help me find me Mum?'

His words were so heartfelt, a lump formed at the back of my throat. I knew I had to leave before emotion got the better of me.

'I will, Thomas. What is her name?'

'Maude. Maude Lander.'

'You wait here, and I'll go and look for her. I'll be back as soon as I can.'

'Thanks, Mister.'

I returned home and retired to bed but was unable to sleep for thoughts about Thomas and his Mum. I needed to find out if she was still alive or not. Penwerris Church was the nearest and most likely candidate for records of birth, marriages and burials, so I arrived there at nine the next morning, just as the vicar turned up to unlock. He left me in the vestry to search through the registers dating back to the 1920's.

I started at 1923 to see if there was any record of Thomas' burial but found nothing for that year, or the two years after. So, he was either buried elsewhere or, possibly, if his body was never found, no burial took place. I decided to give up looking for Thomas' record and looked for his Mum's instead. I turned the page for 1926 and started scanning for Maude Lander. I was shocked to my core when, almost immediately, her name jumped out at me.

Maude Lander (neé Trevaskis) of Falmouth, Buried March 27th 1926. Age 31

Only 31 years old; she probably died of a broken heart after losing her husband and then her son. I wiped away a tear. So many young lives lost in such a short time. I closed the register and went to thank the vicar. On my way home, I pondered how best to deal with the situation. I couldn't change the past, but maybe I could make things better in the present.

'Hello Thomas,' I said.

He stood further down the field than before. His eyes widened and he half-smiled when he saw me. 'Hello Mister. Did you find me Mum?'

I swallowed nervously and hoped I would do this right. 'Not exactly,' I said.

His face fell, so I continued with haste.

'May I ask you a question, Thomas?'

'Yes Mister.'

'Do you know what happens when someone dies?'

'Mum says good people go to heaven, like me Dad.'

'That's right, Thomas. Now I need you to be very brave and listen carefully to what I say.'

'Yes, Mister.'

'Sometimes, when people die unexpectedly, they don't realise they are dead. They don't move on to heaven but linger in the place where they died.'

'Like ghosts you mean?'

'That's right, like ghosts.' I bent down and looked straight into his eyes. 'You see, Thomas, when the rubbish tip slid down, and took you with it... you didn't survive.'

There was an extended silence.

'I'm dead?'

I could hear the fear in his voice so I pressed on. 'Yes, Thomas, but because you didn't realise it, you didn't go to heaven.'

'But what about me Mum?'

'Your mum is in heaven, Thomas. She's waiting for you. So is your dad. You need to go to them.'

Thomas looked around him as if looking for a door or a way to heaven.

'How do I do tha...Mum? Mum!'

A few yards away, the shape of a woman faded into view. She wore a long dress with a white apron over it, her arms outstretched ready to embrace her beloved child. Behind her stood a man dressed in an army uniform.

Thomas ran to her and was swept into her embrace.

Thomas's father placed a hand on his wife's shoulder and the three of them began to fade away. His mum looked at me then smiled and nodded before all three disappeared.

I headed home with tears in my eyes but with lightness in my heart.

For The Love Of Abigail Teague

Ben lagged a few steps behind Simon and Alan as his border collie, Jenny, sniffed something on the ground. He frowned as he listened to them argue over who was the best football team, Manchester United or Leeds United. The two boys were always squabbling. Simon would say something to start Alan off, and Alan would bite every time. Ben wished they would get on better; they were supposed to be friends, after all.

As the boys headed up the winding lane, they passed the gateway to the old ruined house. Jenny barked and tried to pull away from the entrance. Ben looked down the path to the house and noticed movement at a window halfway up the building.

'Look, there's someone at the window of the ruined house,' he said, pointing.

Simon and Alan stopped their arguing and looked first at him then to where he pointed. Through a gap in the tangle of untamed, shadowy Rhododendron and Myrtle trees, they saw part of a tall, stair window. Through the dirt-stained glass they could see the profile of a pale, slender figure. A woman.

She drifted slowly up the stairs, trailing a cloak, or long dress. Jenny whined and pulled on her lead. As the figure passed out of sight, Ben turned to look at Simon, the un-proclaimed leader of this trio of twelve-year olds. Simon was frowning, and his fingers were tapping against his lips. Ben's gaze moved to Alan, whose eyes and mouth were wide open.

'Let's get out of here,' Simon said.

The boys sprinted up the lane, Jenny dragging Ben ahead

of the others. As they poured out onto Woodlane, the early evening August sun blinded them, after the gloomy shade. Somewhere nearby, a radio blared out the latest number-one hit by T-Rex. Jenny kept pulling until they reached the junction of Trelawney Road, where they came to a ragged stop. All three of them gasped for breath. Simon leant against a garden wall then slid down it until he was sat on the floor. Alan bent over, his hands resting on his knees as his body shook.

'It's all right, Jenny,' Ben said, between hastily drawn breaths. 'You're safe now.'

He crouched to stroke her soft black fur, hot beneath his fingers. Jenny looked at him, her tongue panting out the side of her mouth.

'Was that a ghost?' Alan said.

'No, it was just curtains blowing in the breeze,' Simon replied, his expression deadly serious.

'Curtains?' Alan sneered. 'Didn't look like effing curtains to me!'

Simon laughed. 'That's cos it was a bloody ghost, you stupid tosspot.'

'We should tell someone,' Ben said.

'What, like the police or sommin'?' Alan said.

'Maybe, I dunno.' Ben said, scritching the ear of a much calmer Jenny.

Simon laughed again. 'I don't think it's against the law to be a ghost.'

Ben grinned. 'So no trying to get the ghost arrested, then?'

'No point telling our folks either,' Simon said. 'They wouldn't believe us for a minute.'

'Hey, Alan, didn't you once say that your Nana had seen a ghost?' Ben said.

'Yeah. She saw some cousin or other a week after the cousin had died.'

'And doesn't Nana live near here?' Ben asked.

'Budock Terrace. Just over the hill.'

Simon jumped up and, with an exaggerated sweep of his

arm, said, 'Then lead on, Sir Brave Knight. Take us to the kingdom of Budock Terrace so we may consult with the wise Nana.'

Ben noticed Alan's expression harden as if he was about to argue, but instead, he stood tall, puffed out his chest, and purposefully headed off towards Nana's. Simon looked at Ben and gave him a wink, then followed Alan.

Ben shook his head then gave Jenny another scritch behind the ear. 'What are we going to do with those two, Jenny?'

Jenny looked back at him with her beady eyes as if to say, 'No idea, but let's follow them anyway.'

As they neared Nana's house, Alan ran on ahead, opened the big, dark blue door, went in and disappeared from sight.

Ben heard him shout. 'Nana! Nana! We saw a ghost in the ruined house over Woodlane.'

Simon went into the house, but Ben stopped at the threshold.

'Is it all right to bring the dog in?' he called.

Alan was in the kitchen at the other end of the passage, talking excitedly and waving his arms about. 'It...she…was floating up the stairs. She was white and...is it okay if Ben brings Jenny in?'

'Of course 'tis,' Nana said. 'Now will 'ee slow down, Alan, my lad, or you'll do yourself a mischief.'

Alan stopped and let his hands fall to his sides.

'Tha's better. Now why don't 'ee introduce me to your friends?'

Ben entered and closed the front door then led Jenny towards the kitchen. The contents of the house were all old, and the place smelt of wax furniture polish.

Introductions done, Nana said, 'Now then, Alan, tell me again, but slowly, what's all this stuff about a ghost?'

Alan drew a deep breath. 'You know that old ruined house over by Woodlane?'

'The old Hillingdon place? I think abandoned is a more 'propriate term than ruined. It were still standing, last time I looked.'

'We were walking past it, and we saw a lady, in a white dress or sommin', going past the window. Ben saw her first.'

'Did 'ee indeed?' Nana turned to look at Ben.

Ben noticed the deep wrinkles on Nana's face, and the white hair tied back in a bun. She held his gaze for a few seconds then her eyes seemed to focus beyond Ben. She turned to look out of the kitchen window into the back yard, as if an answer was to be found there. Then she quietly said, 'Abi?'

'Abbey?' Alan said. 'Like in Westminster Abbey?'

'No,' Nana said in a dreamy voice. 'Abi, as in Abigail. Abigail Teague.'

'Who's that, Nana? Is she the ghost?'

Nana shook her head and straightened her shoulder. 'Never you mind; you just ignore the ramblings of your old Nana.'

'But Nana...'

'No, my lad, 'tis time you and your friends headed home. Your parents will be wond'rin where you are, and I don't need them coming round 'ere blaming me for keeping you out late.' With that, Nana ushered them out the door, admonishing them. 'Now you go straight home and don't dawdle.'

When they reached the end of Budock Terrace, Ben stopped to let Jenny squat down for a pee. Alan and Simon kept walking.

'Hang on a minute, guys. Jenny needs a wee.'

They stopped and turned around.

'I reckon we should go in have a look around the place,' Simon said.

'Go inside the ruined house?' Alan exclaimed. 'You must be off your effin' rocker.'

'Probably. I do hang around with a knob-head like you, after all.' Simon grinned. 'Okay, we'll do it tomorrow morning. See you there at ten. Bring a torch.'

'And a penknife,' added Ben.

'Good idea.'

'I ain't going in there,' Alan said, folding his arms.

'Then you can stay outside and pee your pants, scaredy cat. See you tomorrow.' Simon turned the corner and headed home.

'I ain't going in, Ben.'

'No-one's forcing you, Alan. You can stay outside and keep watch in case any grown-ups turn up.'

Alan paused, then nodded.

They said their goodbyes and went their separate ways.

Ten o' clock the next morning, the three boys, minus Jenny, met in the lane outside the house. The morning sunshine slipped through the gaps in the trees, it dappled the path and garden. The house seemed much less scary now that it wasn't darkened by shadows. They all looked towards the window, simultaneously hoping for and dreading the ghost's appearance.

'I ain't going in,' Alan declared. 'Ben said I can wait here and keep watch.'

'Bloody good job too,' Simon said. 'Your sissy whining would scare the poor ghost away.'

'Up yours.' Alan stuck two fingers up to Simon.

Ben intervened before the argument got out of hand. 'Alan, if anyone turns up, whistle or shout. You can also go for help if something happens to us. If we're not back in an hour, go tell your Nana.'

Simon headed off down the path. 'Mind how you go Ben,' he called back. 'It's a bit slippery.'

Ben followed, and as they were about to turn left at the end, he looked back at Alan, who shuffled his feet and interwove his fingers, a look of concern on his face. Ben smiled and gave him the thumbs up. A wry smile appeared on Alan's face as he returned the gesture.

It was dark and gloomy under the canopy of unkempt trees and shrubs. Ben realised three things as he and Simon tried to make their way around the house: one, it was much bigger than they realised; two, all the downstairs doors and windows were boarded up; and three, it was almost impossible to get through the overgrown trees and bushes that grew right up to the house. Their clothes and skin got snagged and scratched in the attempt. The smell of decayed flora was overwhelming, but eventually, at the rear of the house, they found a small window about two feet square where the boarding had rotted away. The last remnant hung on by a single rusty nail.

'This looks good.' Simon shone his small torch in through the window. 'I think it's a pantry.'

'Those bits of glass around the window frame don't look so good,' Ben said.

Simon took a small penknife out of his jeans pocket. 'Did you bring your penknife?'

'Yep.' Ben produced his own.

Between them, they quickly dug out the shards of glass from the crumbling, aged putty.

'I'll go first.' Simon put his folded penknife into his pocket and then, holding the torch in his mouth, he grabbed the bottom of the window frame and with a bounce heaved himself headlong through the window. The heels of his shoes clipped the frame before disappearing out of sight. Ben heard some crunching sounds and then Simon's head appeared at the window.

'There's loads of glass on the floor in here. I'll pull you through, so you don't have to put your hands down on it.'

Ben hoisted himself up and onto the window frame. The rough frame scratched his tummy as Simon pulled him through.

When they were both safely inside, they shone their torches around. The light revealed a narrow room with rows of shelving up high, and cupboards below, all green with mould. The odour of damp plaster and rotten wood assailed Ben's nostrils. To his left, at the other end of the room, he noticed an open doorway.

'What a dump,' Simon said.

'Better not hang around. This place feels like it could fall down at any moment. Let's go in there.'

With torches held out in front, they walked, light-footed, through the doorway into a dark kitchen. Ben shone his torch to the left, his eyes tracking the beam. On the outside wall was a door next to a boarded-up window. Below the window was a large porcelain sink set in a long granite worktop. A big wooden table filled most of the floor space. On the other side of the table, a dilapidated Cornish range cooker sat in a large chimney breast.

Ben grimaced. 'Don't reckon there'll be much cooking going on there ever again.'

To their right, a vast Welsh dresser filled the wall next to a closed door. Cobwebs festooned the room like ghoulish Christmas decorations. But although the house seemed unpleasant, Ben didn't feel scared. It wasn't creepy, just old and sad.

Simon walked to the closed door, the beam of his torch pointing towards the door handle. He turned the handled and pulled. The door opened. The hinges complained in a high-pitched creak that made Ben wince.

He followed Simon through the doorway and into the main hallway. It must have been years since anyone had been in the place. The near-end of the hallway was dimly lit by a window, halfway up the staircase. With a shudder, Ben realised that was the where they had seen the ghost the evening before. Simon walked towards the foot of the stairs while Ben stopped and looked around the hallway. He could just make out the front door at the far end. Several doors, all closed, lined the walls of the hallway, except for the near left wall, where the stairs dog-legged around and up.

'What do you reckon, upstairs or downstairs?' Ben said.

'Upstairs,' Simon said. 'But first, wait here.'

Simon started up the stairs, testing each tread before he put his full weight on it. He slowly crept up until he stood on the stair just before the window. He stopped, leant in front of the window, and let out a blood curdling, 'AAAAAARRRGH!'

Ben jumped.

He heard a high-pitched scream from outside, followed a few seconds later by: 'You effin' bastard, I'll effin' kill you.'

Simon burst out laughing then turned and leant against the wall. Tears streamed down his cheeks.

'You should have seen Alan's face. I bet he's pooped himself.'

Ben guiltily joined in with the laughter. 'You really shouldn't be so mean to him. Alan's all right, he is.'

'I know,' Simon replied. 'I guess he just brings out the worst in me. I wouldn't really want to hurt him, but sometimes...'

'I know, easy target.' Ben moved towards the stairs. 'Let's have a look around then get out of here, so Alan can kill you.'

Simon laughed again then ascended the stairs, Ben followed.

The stairs led to a long landing. The upstairs windows hadn't been boarded over, so light shone through the open doorways. Simon switched off his torch and turned left. Ben did the same and they started exploring the rooms. Most of the upstairs rooms were empty. One had a four-poster bed, a wardrobe and a chest of drawers. Another contained a small bed and a dressing table. Pictures hung on the wall. The images faded with time. Ben thought he could make out the shapes of flowers in one and what might have been a landscape in another. In some rooms the wooden floors had collapsed, and they could see into the rooms below. The floor generally didn't feel too solid underfoot.

'Nothing much up here' Simon said. 'Let's go back down.'

Back downstairs, they switched on their torches and started to explore the ground floor rooms, trying each door in turn. Two doors wouldn't open: locked shut or blocked by something on the other side. The rooms they could get in contained the occasional item of furniture or debris from a collapsed floor above, but mainly just peeling paint, cobwebs and mould. They reached the last door on the right and Simon opened it. They shone their torches into the room then froze.

'What the...' Simon said.

Ben was unable to speak. His mind struggled to comprehend what his eyes were seeing.

The room was about twenty-foot square with a big bay window at the far end. Tiny shafts of light pierced through holes in the boards fixed outside. A large ornate fireplace graced the right-hand wall. A huge metal cage filled most of the room, its thick round bars rusted and pitted. The distance from the cage to the walls was just longer than a person could reach. At the near end of the cage, some of the bars formed a door. A door with a big iron mortice lock on it. Inside the cage there was a wooden dining chair and what might have once been some sort of mattress.

Ben came back to his senses, reached in, grabbed the door handle and pulled the door shut.

'Time to go.' he said.

They tried opening the front door, as it was nearest, but it was locked, so they headed back out to the kitchen. The back door was also locked, but the door frame was rotten, so with a few determined yanks on the door handle, Simon managed to pull the lock out of the frame. The boarding on the outside of the door was also rotten, and most of the nails holding it had rusted away. It didn't take much effort for Simon and Ben to push and kick their way out.

Turning right, they continued around the house and headed back to Alan, who greeted them with a disgruntled, 'I'll get you back for that Simon, don't you worry.'

'Okay, I won't worry then,' Simon said.

'You know what I mean.' Alan's face grew serious. 'So, didya see anything?'

'It's pretty much empty,' Ben said, 'apart from a room-sized cage.'

'A cage?'

'With a bed and a chair in it,' Simon said.

'Why would you put a bed and a chair in a cage?'

'No idea,' Ben said. 'Can we go and see your Nana again?'

'You shouldn't ought to break into houses like that,' Nana said. 'It's still trespassin', even if 'tis empty and derelic'. Isn't that right, Papa?'

Alan's Granddad, who sat at the table reading his newspaper, looked up and nodded sagely. 'Ezz 'tis indeed, but boys will be boys, I s'pose.'

'Nana,' Alan said. 'Ben wanted to ask you something.'

'What's that then, Ben?'

'Umm, should I call you Nana?' Ben asked, feeling himself blush.

'Everyone else does, even my 'usband there. Not very often I get called Mrs Angove these days.'

'Well, Nana, do you think there's a connection between the cage and the ghost?'

Nana's lips tightened as she turned her head and stared out of the kitchen window for a few seconds before turning back to him.

''Tis more than likely, yes.'

'Do you think the ghost is the person you mentioned last night? Was it Abigail...?'

'Abigail Teague. If 'tis her, then that cage you found adds an evil twist to an already tragic tale.'

'What happened?'

'We'd better sit ourselves down and get comfy,' Nana pulled out a chair. 'This could take a while.'

They all sat around the table, everybody's attention fixed on Nana. She stared at her hands for a few moments, then released a sigh and looked at each of the boys in turn.

'Abi and I were the same age. We went school together. She was a sweet and kindly girl. There was also a lad, Matty Collins, who was a couple o' years older than Abi and I. He lived in the same street as her, so they were close friends growing up. Well, Matty turned into a fine 'ansom young man, and Abi blossomed into a beautiful young woman. Oh, such a rare beauty she had, inside and out. Friendship became love, and when Matty left school, he promised to marry her as soon as he was able to care for her in the manner she deserved. He gave Abi a silver ring as a token of his love.

'While Abi finished her last couple of years at school, Matty worked at various jobs before ending up as a storeman at the Hillingdon Shipping Company, down by the docks. The Hillingdon family had been in Falmouth for generations. They were a well-regarded family, kind and charitable, until Finn Hillingdon came along. His Mother died when he was a baby, and what with his Father being busy running the company, he was raised by a succession of Nannies. Some of those nannies were strict and cruel, while others spoilt him rotten. Either way, he grew to be a vain, selfish and greedy piece of work.

'When his Father died, Finn took over running the company. He was mean to the crews of his ships, and to the dock workers. Thought nothing of deducting wages for some imagined slight. Any dirty tricks to make more money were fine by him. As Matty was an employee at the same time as he was courting Abi, it weren't long before Finn encountered her. From the moment he first saw her, he wanted her. Not for love, but as a valuable prize to add to his growing fortune. When he learned of their plans for marriage, he came up with a plan of his own, to get Matty out of the way and steal Abi for himself.

'Finn's first move was to offer a well-paid promotion to Matty with a job on board one of his ships. He promised Matty a share in any trading profits, and convinced him that within a couple of years, Matty would have enough money to marry Abi and return to a land-based job. Matty naively jumped at the opportunity, especially when Finn offered to take care of Abi while Matty was at sea.

'And Finn did take care of Abi. She was the only person,

ever, that he was always nice to. He bought her gifts and took her out to places, all to try and win her affections. There was never any impropriety, just Finn behaving as the concerned friend and patron. Whilst he was doing this, he used every trick he could to keep Matty abroad. Making sure the ship only traded between foreign ports, or was held up in a port for some spurious reason. Abi missed Matty terribly, but every so often, she would receive a letter from him, sent from some far-flung place. Matty's words comforted her and kept her love for him strong and true.

'Finn, realising his scheming wasn't working, switched to more desperate measures. He sent a letter, with a bribe, to some corrupt official in the far east and managed to get Matty thrown in jail and forgotten about. He then lied to Abi, saying Matty had died. Abi was grief struck but Finn was always there to comfort and console her. Eventually, Abi fell for his charms and agreed to marry Finn. Unbeknownst to Finn, Matty had escaped from jail and managed to stow away on board a ship heading for England. He was eventually discovered, but when he told the Captain his story, he was allowed to join the crew and work for his passage home.

'As soon as Matty arrived back in port, he headed straight for Abi's family home. It was there he learned of his alleged death and Abi's marriage to Finn. Outraged, Matty threatened to kill Finn, but Abi's father warned against it, saying that killing Finn would only get Matty hung for murder and Abi no better off. Instead, a secret meeting was arranged between Matty and Abi, where they vowed to run away together. Arrangements were made, but news of Matty's return had reached Finn, and when the time came for them to elope, Finn was waiting with a gang of heavies. They beat Matty, then Finn had him arrested and jailed for attempted kidnapping.

'Nothing was seen or heard of Abi again until her death was announced in the paper a few months later. Some round 'ere reckoned Finn had killed her. Others said Finn had imprisoned her in his home and she had died of a broken heart. Judging by the cage you boys discovered, I reckon the latter is true. Anyhow, Finn, unremorseful, died shortly after Abi. He was overseeing the loading of cargo onto one of his ships when the crane's rope broke, and Finn was crushed to death by the load. Some wealthy relative up country inherited all Finn's money but didn't bother with the house, so it was abandoned. Eventually Matty was released from prison, but with the news of Abi's death, he was devastated, a broken man.'

'What happened to him?' Ben asked.

Nana shrugged. 'Probably dead by now.'

'Last I 'eard, he was living up Penryn. Saracen Way, I think,' Papa said.

'You knew him, Papa?'

'Ezz, my bird. Worked with him a few times when I was with Evans Builders. Nice enough chap, good worker, but quiet. Only spoke when spoken to. 'Tis as your Nana says, he was a broken man.'

'So why is Abi still haunting that house?' Simon asked.

'Who knows' Nana said. 'They say some ghosts are afraid to move on to whatever comes next. Others have unfinished business here. Either way, I think it's best if you boys stay away from that house. Not only is it trespassin', it's also dangerous going into a place like that. Who knows what might happen to you?'

Later that day, the boys were back at the empty house. This time, Simon persuaded Alan to come inside with them.

'You should come and see that cage,' he told him. 'You might get to see the ghost as well.'

Alan ummed and ahhed, but eventually agreed. After another complete exploration of the house, the boys ended up in the hallway.

'What do we do now?' Alan asked.

'We wait,' Simon said. 'See if she appears again.'

'What if she does?' Fear edged Alan's voice.

'Then we try and find out what she wants,' Ben said.

As if on cue, the pale figure appeared from the doorway of the caged room, then drifted across the hallway and up the stairs.

'Effin 'ell,' Alan whispered.

'Come on, let's follow her.' Simon headed towards the stairs.

Ben went after him, followed by a reluctant Alan. They slowly crept up the stairs and onto the landing.

'Where is she?' Alan asked.

'In here.' Simon stood at the entrance to one of the rooms.

Ben and Alan joined him, and they saw the figure facing the wall on the far side of the room. Ben thought she looked like she was staring at the faded landscape picture on the wall.

'What's she doing?' Alan said.

'I'm not sure.' Ben walked into the room. 'Hello? Abigail? Can you hear me?'

The ghost didn't respond.

'What do you want?' Ben asked her.

The ghost reached out a hand as if to touch the picture on the wall. She held it there for a few seconds, then faded away.

'She's gone,' Alan said.

''No? Really?' Simon said with sarcasm.

Ben looked down at the room-wide hole in the floor between him and the wall where the ghost had stood.

'Need to get over there,' he said.

'Good luck with that,' Simon said. 'It's too far to jump, and I wouldn't want to land on those floorboards on the other side; they look pretty rotten.'

'Let's go and see if we can find something to bridge the gap,' Ben said.

After a fruitless search for long enough floorboards or beams, they ended up in the kitchen.

'Do you think we could move that table?' Ben said.

'We'd never get it upstairs,' Alan said. 'Not in a million years.'

'I was thinking we could up-end it and lean it against the wall in the room below the one we want.'

'Let's give it a go,' Simon said.

After turning it on its side to get it the through the kitchen door, and with much dragging and a few splinters in their hands, they managed to lean the table upside down against the wall. Using the drawers in the table as steps Ben managed to shin up the table and then gingerly pull himself onto the floor above. He stood up and examined the picture in the fast fading daylight. It was definitely a landscape scene, but he couldn't tell where.

'You pretending to be the ghost now?' Alan said from below.

Ben reached up and gently lifted the picture off the wall

'I'm looking to see if there is anything...here we go.'

'What is it?' Simon asked.

'There's a panel in the wall behind the picture.'

Ben lowered the picture to the floor and leant it against the wall. He examined the panel in the lath and plaster. He pried it open with his penknife and slowly reached into the void behind, wary of traps or spiders. The right side and bottom of the hole were edged by large wooden timbers. He slid his hand to the left side. When he was in it up to his wrist, his fingers brushed up against something cold and smooth. He gently ran his fingers over an object about the size of a hardback novel. Griping it between finger and thumb, he slowly manoeuvred it out. A metal box, rusty in places, but still whole.

'Found anything?' Alan asked.

'Looks like an old biscuit tin.' Ben turned around and crouched down by the hole in the floor. 'Catch. Don't drop it.'

Simon reached up and Ben let the tin fall into his hands.

'Got it.'

'Let's go.' Ben scrambled down the table.

It was dusk as they made their way up onto Woodlane.

They stopped to open the box, in the last rays of sunlight. Alan stood back from it as if expecting something bad to happen.

'You think something is going to jump out and get you, Alan?'

'You never know. Look what happened to that Pandora woman when she opened a box.'

Ben gently lifted the hinged top of the tin box. Inside were several envelopes. Buried beneath them was a tarnished silver ring. Ben lifted the envelopes out and handed them to Simon.

'Here, hold these.'

Simon took them from him and looked at the faded writing on the top envelope. 'Miss Abigail Teague.'

Ben looked at the inner band of the ring. 'M.C and A.T.'

'Matty Collins and Abigail Teague,' Alan said. 'That must be the ring Matty gave to Abi.'

Simon held up the letters. 'And I bet these are the love letters he wrote.'

'Shall we read them?' Alan asked.

'No.' Ben held out the open box for Simon to place the letters in. 'They're none of our business.'

'What we gonna do then?' Alan scratched his head.

'Good question,' Ben said.

The red and grey Grenville bus pulled up at the bus stop by Penryn Post Office.

'Thank you,' Ben said to bus driver as he followed Simon and Alan off the bus. They walked up the ramp onto the high pavement of the main street.

'Which way?' Alan asked.

'That way.' Simon pointed up the street. 'There's a lane there that leads through to a council estate.'

They walked the few yards and turned into the narrow lane. Eventually they came out into a sloping, crescent shaped road.

'Any idea which house?' Alan asked.

'No,' Ben said. 'But we can ask.'

'Ask who? There's no-one here.'

'Yeah, they must have known you were coming and run away,' Simon said.

'Oi, this is too important for you two to turn it into a slanging match.' Ben pointed down the hill. 'Let's try down this way.'

Eventually they met a passer-by, who told them the information they needed to know.

'What if there's no-one home?' Alan said, as the three of them stood in front of a red front door, the paint faded and flaking.

'Then we wait.' Ben raised his fist and knocked on the door.

The door opened to reveal a stooped old man with a bald head and deep-set blue eyes. Eyes that have seen too much sadness, thought Ben.

'Yes? Can I 'elp 'ee?'

'Mr Collins?' Ben asked. 'Matty Collins?'

'Yes, tha's right,' he said.

'My name is Ben. This is Simon and this is Alan. We've come to talk to you about Abigail Teague.'

A look of sorrow passed over Matty's face.

''Ave 'ee indeed?' Matty said.

'We've found this tin with some letters and a ring in it.'

The old man's face grew suspicious. He peered at Ben.

'We found them in the old Hillingdon house.' Ben offered the tin.

The man jerked back at the mention of the name Hillingdon, but recovered himself and glanced down at the tin. Ben noticed tears forming at the corners of the man's eyes.

'You'd better come on in then. Come in, and be welcome.'

Matty Collins and the three boys stood in the hallway of the old house. Matty clutched the ring in one hand and the letters in the other.

'There.' Ben pointed to the figure drifting from the caged room towards the stairs.

'Abi?' Matty said, stepping towards the figure.

The figure paused, then turned towards Matty, becoming more substantial as the gap between them closed. She was wearing a long white dress, high-waisted and cinched with a bow. Long dark hair cascaded in ringlets and framed the most beautiful face Ben had ever seen.

'She is so beautiful,' Alan whispered.

'Yes...' Simon confirmed.

Ben smiled to himself. Finally, they agreed about something.

'Oh, my precious Abi,' Matty said, as he stood face to face with her.

Ben noticed that the years had fallen from Mr Collins, revealing glimpses of the young man he had once been.

He felt they were intruding on something very personal and private, so he nudged Simon and Alan and nodded back towards the kitchen. With unspoken agreement, they left Matty and Abi to their reunion.

Simon sat leaning against the gatepost. Ben and Alan stood in the gateway, looking towards the house.

Matty appeared through the overgrown garden. As he approached, his eyes no longer looked sad, and he walked much more upright.

'Everything okay, Mr Collins?' Ben asked.

Matty smiled, his grateful, happy gaze penetrating Ben's eyes.

'Everything is jus' fine, Master Ben. Thank you.' His eyes moved to Alan and Simon. 'Thank you all.'

'What about the ghost...I mean, Abi?' Alan blurted, his hands gesticulating wildly.

'She's gone, and, the Lord willin', I won't be far behind,' Matty said.

'Gone where?' Alan asked.

Simon stood up from the gatepost and put his arm around Alan's shoulder. 'Just gone, Alan, and we must go too, old buddy of mine. Why don't we take Mr Collins to see your lovely Nana? Let them catch up on old times.'

Alan put his arm around Simon's shoulder, and with a smile, replied, 'Yeah, lets. Old buddy of mine.'

A wave of joy radiated through Ben as he watched the two of them head off up the lane together.

He gestured for Matty to follow them. 'After you, Mr Collins.'

Patch

There's that ship that Mrs Lanston pointed out to us on our school trip to the Docks. It's been there ages, but it's off to sea at last. Must've needed lots of repairs. Fixed proper now though, 'cos jeeps, it's moving fast. Wonder where it's off to? America? Africa? Japan? Wonder if I could swim after it? Go to Gylly beach and dive into the water. Swim to Japan. Meet some Samurai and climb Mount Fuji then Swim back home again. Haha! That'd be a laugh. Imagine telling the kids at school. Probably be in the Falmouth Packet: "Eight-year old Timmy Jago swims to Japan and back."

The sea's dark. Those clouds are shifting on. Wonder if that ship's gonna hit the coming storm? Winds deffo getting up. The oak tree's branches are dancing like mad, all except that broken branch, the one I snapped earlier. Can't believe I fell. Lucky I didn't hurt myself. It's a big drop. What, twenty feet, maybe? That branch must've broken my fall. Shook me up though. Lucky Mum didn't see. She would've given me hell if I'd hurt myself. Funny that, you hurt yourself and Mum gives you a clip round the ear.

Grass is getting long. I expect Dad will cut it soon. He doesn't normally let it get this long. It's getting dark. Must've been sat here for ages.

What's that? Something moving behind the bushes. What is it? There. By the oak tree. A dog. A springer. With a red and blue ball in its mouth. Patch's ball? Patch? 'Patch?'

He's coming. Running. He's wagging his tail in a circle, the way he does. He's dropped the ball. He's jumping. He's in my arms. Licking my face. I always said he was the lickiest dog ever.

'Oh Patch. You're the best. Love you, Patch.'

His coat is so soft and silky. He's wriggling. He wants to get down.

'Down you go then. You wanna play?'

He's gone for the ball.

'Wanna catch the ball, Patch?'

Oh no, here we go, doing his tease thing. Ball between his paws. Head down, nose almost touching the ball. Bum in the air. Tail circling. I love that cute growl of his. Better try and get the ball off him then. Slowly does it. Crouch down. Reach out. Nearly there. Dammit, too slow. He's running to the other end of the lawn. Haha, same move; drop ball, crouch, growl. Better try again. Maybe if I ignore him, and walk to the side of him, I can catch him out. Nearly there. Don't look at him. Ready and... now. Too slow again. There he goes, lap of honour round the lawn.

'Come on, Patch. If you don't give me the ball, I can't throw it for you.'

Ooo that worked, he's dropped the ball right at my feet. I love the way his tongue hangs out the side of his mouth when he pants. Right, throw the ball up as high as possible. Not bad, must be thirty feet up. He's prancing around on his back legs, getting ready to jump. Oh no, the wind has blown the ball towards the house.

'Get it, Patch.'

The ball's bounced. Wow, not bad. Must be five feet up. There's Patch the springy springer flying through the air. Reckon he's got kangaroo blood in him.

'Nice catch, Patch.'

Nearly dark now. Patch is looking towards the house. The lights are on inside. Mum's stood at the kitchen window, crying. I turn away and look for Patch.

Where's he going now? He's sniffing around the oak tree. He's barking at me.

'What's up, Patch?'

He's like that Lassie dog in the movies; when she's telling

the Sheriff where the bad guys are hiding.

'What you trying to say, Patch?'

Another bark. He's looking away, towards the bushes. Now back at me.

'You gotta go, Patch? You leaving again?'

My tummy feels strange. This isn't right. Patch died last year. We buried him with his ball. Acute pancri-something the vet said.

I look at him. He barks and stands on his back legs, front legs scrabbling at the oak tree.

'Is there something up there, Patch?'

Can't see much in the darkness, apart from the splintered end of that branch I broke. That's a long way up. Or down. A long way to fall. Really can't believe I didn't hurt myself.

Mum's still crying in the kitchen, only now Dad's there too, with his arm around her.

The strange feeling in my tummy's gone.

'I have to come with you, don't I, Patch?'

Patch does his circular tail wags. Barks.

'Okay, Patch. Let's go.'

The Black Cap

The applause faded, the story teller stepped off the low stage and a murmur of voices rippled through the dimly lit room as the audience discussed the tale that had been told. Thirty people, sat around nine card tables, squeezed into the upstairs room of the Falmouth Labour Club for the Inky Fingers Writing Group's monthly get together. It was 'Creep, Scare and Shock' night. Flickering light from nubs of candles placed around the room, gave the already gloomy place an eerie feel. Worn, red curtains were drawn over the large sash windows at the front of the building. Red flock wallpaper framed the doorway on the rear wall.

In the front row, by the window to the right of the stage sat Dave, the founder and host of the group, chatting to his girlfriend, Linda. In the centre, avid supporters Geoff and Molly, the fifty-something couple, who never missed a session, giggled, heads close together. To their right three tables of college students, debated the last story and sipped slowly at their half pints of cheap lager. Two of them had already read their stories that evening, also to polite applause. At the centre table in the back row, Zena Williams, entertainment correspondent from the local paper, scribbled notes for the article she was doing on the Inky Fingers Writing Group. Next to her, in the gloom of the back-right corner, three scruffy, long-haired young men, clearly under the influence of alcohol and more, laughed over-loudly at each other's jokes. One of them, banged his pint glass on the wooden table and demanded that someone go downstairs to the bar and fetch him another, given that the drinks that night were on him. Why should he go down the steep, rickety stairs? They weren't part of the usual crowd, but on a Tuesday night entertainment in town was limited and one of them was clearly flush with cash. The rest of the audience consisted of the evening's story tellers and their entourages.

Dave was about to stand and announce the next speaker when a voice, brittle with age, said, 'I was dead, and looking down at my body, cold and useless on the floor.'

The words were quietly spoken but every ear in the room heard them; all conversation ceased and, as one, the audience turned their faces towards the stage. A slight figure, a woman, hunched, concealed in a floor-length hooded cloak. The dark velvet shimmered in the soft light. The shadow of the hood obscured her face as she spoke again.

'The skin on what was once my face looked waxy, with a bluish undertone, like the last fading remnants of a bruise. The furrows of experience no longer lined my forehead. A hint of a pout on my lips, as if I was about to speak.'

The audience froze into a tableau, transfixed. The speaker left a pause that bordered on the uncomfortable, then continued.

'And what of the circumstances of my death? I had just returned home from my usual evening stroll along Greenbank Terrace, where I live, alone. As I closed the front door, a noise from behind me alerted my attention, and I spun around, just in time to see a chef's knife glint in the light before it was thrust into my stomach.'

The reporter, reaching for her glass, stopped mid-reach. The students, wide-eyed, paid the woman an attention their tutors would surely envy.

'Unbearable pain tore through me as I felt the knife slice through my guts. My legs turned to jelly, and I started to fall. A dark clad figure withdrew the blade and thrust it again and again, into my midriff and chest. The blade grated against bone as it passed between my ribs. I tried to scream, but my punctured lungs were unable to draw breath.'

Geoff and Molly, mouths agog, clutched each other's hand

protectively, unprepared for such graphic detail.

Overcome by fear and shock, adrenalin coursed through my body, dulling the pain. I looked at my attacker's face. He was adult, but barely. Lank, greasy hair emerged from under a black flat cap. Cruel eyes stared at me, an evil sneer upon his lips. The stench of stale beer and tobacco enveloped him. I tried to ask him 'why' but before my breathless lips could form the question, darkness overtook my mind and I collapsed to the floor.'

Silence reverberated around the room as the speaker paused for a few seconds. The audience's senses were in overdrive, as if they were reliving the story. Dave turned to Linda, wondering if they should stop the speaker, but Linda was oblivious to everything apart from the hooded figure and her abhorrent tale and before Dave had chance to ask, the aged voice continued.

'The next thing I knew, I was looking down at my face looking back up at me from the hallway floor, the 'why' of it all still evident in my final expression. A dark stain of blood spread through my coat and oozed out onto the carpet. My attacker put the knife in his coat pocket and crouched down beside me. He took my left hand in his, and with his right tried to pull off the gold and bejewelled rings on my fingers. I had been murdered for my rings. Rings I had been determined to own and had spent a lifetime accruing. Rings trapped behind finger joints swollen with age and arthritis.

Realising the futility of his efforts, he proceeded to bend my fingers back, one by one, until each one popped at the knuckle joint with a resounding crack. Reaching into his coat pocket, he retrieved his knife and sawed his way through the skin, muscle and tendons of my broken fingers. Blood coated the blade and my rings. With the fingers now separated from my hand, he tried to remove my rings from the severed ends, but the flare of the bone still hampered his efforts. So instead, he gathered up the bloodied digits and put them in his coat pocket.'

In the back, right corner of the room, a chair grated slowly across the floor as its drunken occupant slid it away from the table.

'After removing the fingers from my left hand, the murderer repeated the ghastly deed on my right hand, leaving me with these.' She pulled her arms out from under her cloak and held up two, bloody, fingerless hands.

Several people in the audience screamed. Molly fainted against Geoff.

The woman stared straight out into the audience, directing her gaze at the group of three drunken young men at the back of the room.

'Was it worth it, I wonder?' she said.

One of the men lurched up from his chair and staggered erratically across the room, knocking Zena, the reporter, to the floor as he passed. Her surprised yell drew the audience's attention. Heads turned and everyone's gaze followed the man's flight across the room. He banged his head on the doorframe in his drunken haste, and a black flat cap fell to the floor.

As he disappeared through the doorway, mental jigsaw pieces fell into place. The audience heard a shocked yell and a series of thumping sounds, then a moment's silence that seemed to last forever, followed by a blood curdling crack as something hit the floor at the bottom of the stairs. A roomful of stunned faces turned back towards the now empty stage.

Lady of the Ladder

It was mid-afternoon on Saturday 2nd August 1975, two days after my thirteenth birthday. I was stood at The Moor in Falmouth, at the bottom of Jacob's ladder, about to start climbing the 111 steps to go see Nana, who lived on Wellington Terrace near the top of the ladder. I had climbed these steps many times, and hated the ordeal every time. Climbing the steps made my legs ache. They always felt a bit wobbly by the time I got to the top.

The ladder had been built by Jacob Hamblen in the 1840's as a short cut between his home at the top and his business at the bottom. Better if he had built a cable car from my house on The Beacon to Nana's, and saved me the slog up the ladder. I placed my foot on the first step and began the climb. To relieve the monotony, I broke the 111 steps up into sections: 9 steps, long landing, 5 steps, short landing, 44 steps, short landing, 32 steps short landing, 16 steps, short landing, 5 steps, 36 paces up the lane, done. I had just counted the 44 steps and reached the short landing, where a lane branches off to the left up to Vernon Place, when I was interrupted by a female voice.

'Hello, Charles Pascoe.'

Startled, I looked around for the source of the voice. There, in the shadow of the wall that runs up the right-hand side of the ladder, stood a lady. She had a pretty face and looked about twenty, but was dressed in dark clothing that seemed old fashioned, a bit like the clothes ladies wore in some of the black and white films on telly. Wary, and heeding my Mum's warning about not talking to strangers, I looked up the lane to Vernon Place, checking for an escape route just in case.

'Off to Nana's, are you?' The lady continued 'You might want to think about going the long way around via Vernon Place, because Stewart Holman and his gang are up top waiting for you.'

Stewart Holman was the school bully who I had been avoiding all week, following an incident where I made him look even more stupid than normal and he ended up being marched to the headmaster's office.

His parting words to me as Mr Watson, the science teacher, dragged him away by the scruff of the neck were, 'I'm gonna kill you 'til you're dead!'

'Instead of killing me until I'm alive?' I answered, which was probably not a good idea for a response, but I couldn't resist.

All the kids in the playground watching the event burst out laughing. Even Mr Watson had joined in.

I was wondering how Stewart Holman knew I would be here, when the lady spoke again.

'Andrew Long told him you go to your Nana's every Saturday afternoon. And no, I can't read your mind, but I can read the expression on your face.'

Andrew Long lived on my road. We used to play together through Infant and Junior school, but when we got secondary school, Andrew ended up in the same class as Stewart and eventually joined Stewart's gang.

'Thanks for the warning, Mrs...' I said.

'Miss. Miss Maggie Trecombe. I went to school with your Papa Clive.'

I knew this couldn't be true, because Papa was in his mid-fifties, but I didn't say anything. Turning towards Vernon Place, I said thank you again and waved goodbye.

As I walked away Maggie said, 'Bye Charles. Give your Papa my regards.'

I took the long way round, as suggested, and when I got the end of Wellington Terrace, I could hear Stewart's gang shouting and hollering down by the top of Jacob's Ladder, so I sprinted as fast as I could to Nana's and shot in the front door. Nana and Papa were sat in the front room: Papa in his big chair watching horse racing on the telly; Nana on the settee reading a magazine.

'Hello love,' Nana said. 'Everything all right? Did you have a nice birthday?'

'Brill thanks, Nana. Thanks for the presents. They're great.'

'You're welcome.' Nana got up from the settee. 'I'll go and put the kettle on and make your Papa a cup of tea. You want some lemonade and congress tarts? I bought them 'specially for you?'

'Yes please, Nana.'

Nana headed out of the room and off down the passage to the kitchen.

'Papa?'

'Yes, my bird?'

'Do you know a Maggie Trecombe?'

Papa pondered for a moment then replied, 'That's a name I haven't heard in a long time. There was a Maggie Trecombe when I was young. She was killed in the war. The Methodist Chapel got hit when the German's bombed the town back in 1940. Maggie was coming up Jacob's Ladder when it happened. She was killed in the explosion. Why do you ask, son?'

'I just seen her down the ladder. She said she went school with you.'

''Ezz, that she did.' Papa stood up and turned off the telly. 'But she's been dead over 30 years, so it won't be the same person you saw. What did she look like?'

'About twenty years old. Very pretty. Dark hair, swept back and up. Wearing old fashioned clothes.'

Papa frowned. 'That sounds like Maggie Trecombe, all right.'

'What sounds like Maggie Trecombe?' Nana said, walking into the room carrying a tray ladened with congress tarts, a glass of lemonade, a teapot and other crockery.

'The boy said he's just seen Maggie Trecombe down the ladder. Told him she went school with me.'

'Well if it was her, I'd be telling you to stay well away from her. A nasty piece of work she was.' Nana plonked the tray on the table a little too forcefully, causing the contents to bounce and clatter.

'You knew her too, Nana?'

'No, thankfully. Well, I didn't know her like your Papa did, but everyone knew her by reputation. Thieving, lying, trouble making bitch she was. 'Scuse my French.'

Nana put a tea strainer on a cup and started pouring tea from the teapot. 'Most people round here reckoned it was divine right when she got killed.'

'She seemed nice enough to me.' I said. 'Saved me from some...err, bother.'

'Well, it can't be her, now can it,' Nana handed me the lemonade and a tea-plate with two congress tarts on it, 'what with her being dead all these years? Probably someone playing a joke on you.'

'Or it could be her ghost,' Papa said.

'Ghost?' Lemonade splashed my shorts as a shiver ran down my spine.

'T'ain't no such thing as ghosts,' Nana snapped. 'Don't you go filling the boy's head with stuff and nonsense. You'll give him nightmares. Let's talk about something else.'

The conversation moved on to other things, but I couldn't stop thinking about the woman. Was she a ghost? Or was it as Nana said, someone playing a joke on me?

I went home via Trelawney Road and Berkeley Vale, just in case Stewart Holman was still hanging around Jacob's Ladder. So it wasn't until the following Saturday that I made my way back up the ladder. Thankfully, Stewart Holman had forgotten about me by then and moved onto other prey so I felt safe going to Nana's that way. When I reached the landing where I'd encountered the woman the week before, no-one was there.

I looked around, then called her name softly, 'Miss Trecombe?'

'Hello, Charles.'

I jumped as she suddenly appeared in exactly the same place as before.

'Thanks for helping me last week,' I said. I felt a mixture of apprehension and curiosity.

'You're most welcome. Any more problems with Stuart Holman?'

'No, I've managed to avoid him all week, but I'm sure he'll be after me again. I seem to have a knack for annoying him.'

She laughed.

Umm, Miss Trecombe?'

'Please, call me Maggie.'

'Maggie, can I ask you something?'

'Anything you like.'

'Papa said you were killed here by a bomb in 1940.'

'He's right. I was on the third step down from where you're standing now when the bomb went off. That dealt me a mighty blow. Then I bounced down a few steps, which finished me off.'

'So are you...umm, are you a ghost?'

'That's as good a word as any to use.'

I paused for a moment, not sure whether to believe her, or what to say next. It was difficult to take in the fact that I might be talking to a ghost.

She smiled. 'Not convinced? How about this?'

With that, she disappeared. Then immediately reappeared further up the steps.

My jaw dropped. I stood there, stunned.

She laughed. 'Better close your mouth or you might start catching flies.'

I closed my mouth and she disappeared again then reappeared in front of me.

'That proof enough for you?' she said, smiling.

'Err, yeah.'

'You might want to keep quiet about it. Might not look too good if you start telling people you've seen a ghost.'

'No. I mean yes. Well, err, thanks again.' I hurried off up the steps to Nana's.

'Bye, Charles,' she called out behind me.

'Bye,' I shouted, without looking back.

I didn't say anything to Nana and Papa, but my mind was awhirl with questions. I spent the whole week thinking about her. Whilst it was a bit scary, I felt quite chuffed that I knew a ghost. No-one else I knew had a ghost of their own, especially one as pretty as Maggie.

The next Saturday couldn't come around quick enough. I wolfed down my lunch and headed off to Nana's earlier than usual. As I ran up the steps of the Ladder, I forgot all about my usual step counting, too busy looking to see if she was there. When I was a few steps from the landing, she appeared. I stumbled, and just managed to stop myself falling by grabbing the handrail.

'More speed, less haste, Charles,' she said smiling.

'Yes, Miss Tre...Maggie.'

'In a rush, and earlier than usual? I'm flattered such a handsome young man is so keen to see me. Hasn't happened in a very long time.'

I felt myself blush. She laughed. Her laugh was nicer than chocolate.

She looked at me intently for a few seconds. 'Come on then, out with them. I can see you have a million questions to ask, so fire away.'

'Maggie, why are you here?'

'To seek redemption.'

'What does that mean?'

'When I was alive, I was a very bad person. I did terrible things, which caused hurt and suffering to a lot of people. When I died, instead of going on to wherever good people go after death, I remained here. And here I must stay until I have done enough good to make up for the bad I did in life.'

'Did someone tell you that?'

'No, I just know it. Don't ask me how, but from the instant I returned, I knew that was my lot.'

'How long will it take until you are redempted?'

'Redeemed,' she said with a chuckle. 'I have no idea. As long as it takes.'

'How will you know when you've finished?'

'I won't be here anymore.'

I stared at the ground for a few moments and thought about what she had said.

'What sort of bad things did you do?' I asked.

'Too many things to mention. If it's considered a sin, I've probably done it. As a little girl, I learnt to lie and cheat to get what I wanted. As I grew up, I found other ways to benefit myself at the expense of others.'

'Have you ever murdered someone?'

'Not directly. I've never actually killed someone, but through my words and deeds, people have ended up dead.'

'How?'

'Before the war, there was a young married couple expecting their first child. They lived not far from here, with the wife's Mother, but were saving every penny from the money the husband earned to afford a place of their own. I stole their money. To make up for the loss, the husband took to working every hour he could, which exacted a terrible toll on him. He was always exhausted, and often ill. Just before the child was born, he had nearly earned and saved enough to realise their dream, but his tiredness made him careless at work and he died in an accident. If I hadn't stolen the money, he wouldn't have died, and the family would have lived happily ever after.'

'What did you do with the money?'

'Gambled it, drank it away, used it to get what I wanted: bets, booze, and bribes.' She sighed and looked down. 'Much good it did me, stuck on these steps until whenever.'

'You can't leave the Ladder?'

'Nope. Can't go past the top or bottom step or up the path to Vernon Place.' She looked up towards Vernon Place longingly.

'Have you tried?'

'No.'

'Then how do you know you can't leave?'

She reached out her left arm and pointed at the stone wall that ran the length of the Ladder. 'Can you walk through this wall?'

'No, of course not.'

She gave me a stern look. 'Have you tried?'

'No.'

Her stern look softened to a smile. 'Then how do you know you can't walk through it?'

I held my hands up in mock submission and smiled back at her.

'Okay, you got me. But how can you redeem yourself if you're stuck here? How can you do good things?'

'It's not s'posed to be easy, but every so often, I get the chance.'

'Like what?'

'Like telling you about Stewart Holman, which probably saved you from being beaten up. Hopefully, that counts in my favour.'

I thought about what she'd told me. 'If there's anything I can do to help you,' I said, 'I will.'

'Thank you, Charles. I'll bear it in mind.'

The first opportunity to help her came the following week. We were stood on the landing, talking, when suddenly she said, 'Visitors.'

I looked down the Ladder and saw two men coming up towards us. They were laughing and joking with each other.

'Right, Charles, that's Mike Basset and Andy Dawe. I need to you to ask Mike if he remembered the prescription.'

'What prescription?'

'Never mind. Just go down and ask him, then keep going

down. Will you do that for me, please?'

The concerned look on Maggie's face convinced me, and I started down the steps.

As I drew near to the men, who were busy talking, I paused and said, 'Hope you remembered the prescription, Mr Basset?' Then without waiting for his response, I carried on down the Ladder.

'Eh what?' I heard Mike say behind me. 'Oh bugger it. I forgot the wife's pills. I better go back to the chemist's and get them. I'll see you tomorrow, Andy.'

I hurried across the Moor and waited outside the library, watching as Mike walked around the corner from the Ladder and into Killigrew Street. The chemist's shop was only a few doors up. He went into the shop, and reappeared a few minutes later. As he started back up the Ladder, I followed. By the time I got back to Maggie, he was out of sight at the top.

'How did you know about the prescription?' I asked.

'Just a hunch. That and knowing how men's minds work.'

'And how's that?'

'Mike and Andy go to the bookies every Saturday to bet on the horses. When they came down this morning, I heard Mike say that he mustn't forget his wife's prescription as she ran out this morning and if she don't take it regular she'll suffer for it later. Seeing them coming back happy told me they'd won on the horses, and probably forgotten everything else, like prescriptions.'

I looked at her in awe. 'You're amazing, Maggie.'

'Aww, thank you, Charles, but I couldn't have done it without your help.'

'Why not? Why couldn't you just tell him?'

'Because most people, specially grownups, tend not to see what they don't believe exists.'

'"T'aint no such thing as ghosts," that's what Nana says.'

'Exactly. Which makes me think you'd best not stand there talking to me. If anyone looks this way, they're most likely to see you talking to yourself. Go sit yourself down over there.'

She pointed to the path up to Vernon Place. I went a couple of paces up the path, sat down and leant against the wall.

'If anyone comes, I'll say "visitors" and you can make yourself scarce.'

'Okie dokie, Maggie.'

That's how it was with my visits from then on. I would sit down against the wall, out of sight from anyone on the Ladder. Usually, I took a comic or pocket sketchpad with me, so when Maggie said "visitors" I pretended to read or draw.

One Saturday, a couple of years later, I had just turned the corner by the Methodist Chapel at the bottom of the Ladder when I noticed two old ladies, both loaded with shopping bags, slowly making their way up the ladder a short distance ahead of me. One was Patty Harris, who worked in the corner shop at the end of Nana's road. The other was Mrs Oates, a widow and a friend of Nana and Papa. I knew Patty quite well from visits to the shop. She was always kind to me, doing things like putting in a few extra sweets when I went in for a quarter of mint imperials. Mrs Oates was much more serious, usually just saying a gruff hello whenever I saw her. When they reached Maggie's landing, they turned up towards Vernon Place, the top flights of steps probably too much for them to manage.

I saw Maggie before I reached the landing and noticed a worried look on her face.

Before I had a chance to speak she said, 'Quickly, Charles, go after them and bring them back. I need to see them, and for them to see me.'

'How am I going to...'

'I'm sure you'll think of something, go on now.'

I hurried after the ladies, and just before they turned into Vernon Place, I called out. 'Excuse me, ladies.'

They both stopped and turned. Patty smiled when she saw me. Mrs Oates just gave me a stony stare.

'Hello, Charles,' Patty said. 'You all right? How's your grandparents?'

'Fine, thanks.'

'Good, good. What can we do for you?'

My mind raced trying of think of something to say. 'Umm, could you come back down here, please? I need to show you something.'

'Show us what?' Mrs Oates said. 'Why should I wear out my poor old legs just for you?'

'Please,' I begged, trying my best to look desperate.

'What's up, Charles? Patty's smile changed to a look of concern. 'Is something the matter?'

'No, I just... I... I need you to see someone. Please. Just down by the Ladder. I'll carry your bags for you.'

'No, need.' Patty turned to Mrs Oates. 'Come on, Babs, let's see what this is all about.'

Mrs Oates let out an exasperated sigh. 'All right, all right, but if this is some kind of a joke, I'll be telling your grandparents. Here, take my bags, you can carry them home for me after.'

'I will, Mrs Oates. No problem.'

I turned and walked back down towards Maggie, who was stood in the middle of the landing with her hands by her sides. When I reached the end of the path, I turned and waited for Patty and Mrs Oates. They stopped a few feet away from me. Maggie smiled at me as if to say, well done.

'Right then, Charles, here we are,' Patty said. 'Now what, or rather who, is this all about?'

'Do you remember Maggie Trecombe?' I asked.

At the mention of her name both their expressions turned less friendly.

'What about her?' Patty said. 'She's been dead for years.'

'Dead and burning in hell, hopefully,' Mrs Oates added.

'Umm, not quite,' I said, 'Do you remember what she looked like?'

'I'll never forget that face,' Mrs Oates said. 'I've wanted to punch it often enough after she helped my hubby to an early grave from boozing.'

'Well,' I said, 'she's stood right behind me.'

'What?'

Both ladies looked past me. I knew they could both see Maggie because their eyes went wide. As I stepped to one side, Patty's hand went to her mouth and she whispered, 'Oh, my sainted aunt.'

Mrs Oates' reaction was rather different. She spat at Maggie's feet, then said, 'Come back to spread some more of your evil, have you, bitch?'

'Hello Patricia, Hello Barbara,' Maggie said. 'I have some things I need to tell you both.'

'There's nothing you have to say that I want to hear.' Mrs Oates folded her arms, apparently unphased by the fact that she was talking to a ghost. 'And if it's forgiveness you're after, you can forget it.'

'Now, now.' Patty reached out and laid her hand on Mrs Oates arm. 'The Lord said we should always forgive those that trespass against us.'

'I don't seek, or deserve, your forgiveness,' Maggie said. 'Patty, I won't mention names, but you were led to believe that I had an affair with your husband. This is not true. Your husband has never been, or would ever be, unfaithful to you.'

'You would say that though, wouldn't you?' Mrs Oates said.

'Barbara,' she said to Mrs Oates, 'I have been dead for thirty-five years. I have nothing to gain by lying to either of you.'

'I believe you,' Patty said, staring hard at Maggie, as though trying to decide whether she could trust her own eyes and ears or not. 'Thank you for saying so.'

Maggie smiled at Patty and turned back to Mrs Oates. 'Barbara, your hatred of me is more than justified. I helped your husband on the road to ruin through booze. His early death is part of the reason I am doomed to haunt this place. Now, this might sound strange, but do you have a creaky stair at home?'

'I don't see what that has to do with anything.'

'I am merely suggesting that it might be to your advantage to lift the stair tread.'

'Is that it?' Mrs Oates said. 'Can we go now?'

'Yes,' Maggie said. 'Thank you for listening.'

'Come on then, Patty, let's go. Charles, bring those bags.'

I looked at Maggie, who smiled at me and gave a quick nod of her head.

I found out later that Mrs Oates had lifted the creaky stair and found a stash of money and jewellery. The money was no longer legal tender, but the jewellery was quite valuable. I asked Maggie how she knew about it.

'Jack Oates and I were staggering home drunk one night when he said to me that a creaky stair had a lot of uses. He winked, and said that one of those uses was letting you know if there was an intruder in the house. I guessed another use would be to hide valuables. I was going to break into their house and find out, but a certain German bomb put paid to that idea.'

'I see.'

'Did you know Barbara Oates is a relative of your nemesis, Stuart Holman?

'No, really?'

'His dad's aunt. Do you still have problems with Stuart?

'Not anymore. Not since he said he heard I had a girlfriend, but she was so ugly I wouldn't let anyone see her. So, I punched him and gave him a bleeding nose. He has left me alone since then.'

'That was very chivalrous of you, my brave knight.'

My friendship with Maggie continued, with me helping out with her redemption when I could. Until one day, several years later, when I was in the middle of taking my final A-level exams, I popped up the Ladder to see her. She looked so happy as I said hello.

'Charles, it's done. I can go.'

Confused, I asked, 'Go where?'

'Beyond, where good people go when they die.'

'How do you know?'

'I can feel it. A sense of freedom.'

'So why haven't you gone?'

'Because I had to say goodbye to my handsome young man first.'

My face grew hot. 'Oh, right.'

'Thank you, Charles, for your help. And for believing in me.'

'You're welcome, Maggie.'

'But most of all, thank you for being my friend.'

She started to fade, and tears welled in my eyes. 'Thank you too, Maggie. I'll miss you.'

'Don't worry, Charles. We will definitely meet again. Just not in this world.'

And with that, she was gone. I pondered her words for a few moments, smiled and headed on up to Nana's.

Night Time At Nana's

Adrian knew there was something in the room with him. He could feel it. A bad thing that meant him harm. Where exactly IT was, he couldn't quite tell, but it was definitely there. He pulled the bed covers tighter over his head, hoping he was safe under the cotton sheet, heavy woollen blanket and candlewick bedspread.

Outside, the wind howled and whined through the electric wires across the road, the sound muffled by the bedding. The large sash window rattled in its wooden frame. Rain pelted against the glass. Was IT hiding in the window frame, getting ready to make the window fall in on him causing broken shards to stab him to death? Maybe IT would wait until he was asleep then open the window and let the wind, rain and more bad things in to get him. He scrunched up into a ball. The sheets felt stiff and rough against his face and feet. His nylon pyjamas made the rest of him hot and sweaty; the shiny material clung to his skin. He noticed that the smell under the bedclothes had changed; the fresh aroma of Nana's washing powder replaced by stale air. He must have been under the covers for a long time. Maybe he should come up for air, but then IT might get him. But if he stayed under the covers, he might suffocate.

He screwed his eyes shut tight, threw back the covers and sat up. Cool, fresh air washed over him, carrying the sickly-sweet smell of wax polish with it.

Outside, the wind gusted harder, almost as if it knew Adrian was no longer under the covers. A surge of rain hit the window as if to say, 'IT is coming for you.'

Part of Adrian's mind screamed, 'Don't look, don't look.' Another part whispered, 'Open your eyes and look.' Daring him. Urging him. His mind became a battle of wills between the two thoughts, building to a crescendo until he thought his head would explode.

Adrian loved being at Nana and Papa's during the daytime. They both spoiled him rotten with sweets and fizzy drink. If he was staying the night, Nana would cook whatever dinner he wanted. Breakfast was as many Weetabix and as much buttered toast as he could eat. He would go on long walks with Nana around the sea front, or Papa would take him to Kimberley Park, pushing Adrian high into the air when he was on the swing. Night-time at Nana's was not so nice. Both grandparents went to bed at seven o' clock and turned the lights out shortly after, therefore Adrian had to as well. Since he started junior school last year, Mum and Dad let him stay up until eight o'clock; nine o'clock during the holidays. The worst thing about staying at Nana's was having to sleep in the spare bedroom. The room was tiny, barely six-foot wide and nine-foot long. At one end, the door opened outwards onto the landing. The head of the single bed was against the wall beside the doorway. The bed took up most of the length of the room. A few feet in from the doorway squatted a dark wood dressing table with an overly large mirror attached. Next to that stood a small matching wardrobe. Thick, dark brown curtains dominated the far end of the room. At night, the room and its contents became the scariest place he had ever known.

Adrian opened his eyes.

Absolute blackness.

A jolt of fear ran through him. IT could be right there in front of him, ready to attack. He held his breath then slowly released as his eyes adjusted to the darkness. He could make out the white flower pattern on the wallpaper. He avoided looking directly at the flowers; if he stared at them long enough, he knew he would see grotesque faces form amongst them. Maybe IT was hiding there, in the wallpaper right above his head, watching and waiting. Ready to jump out of the wallpaper and land right on top of him. He froze.

Nothing.

The outline of the dressing table and wardrobe came into view. A shiver ran down Adrian's back as he looked at the mirror, expecting to see a face appear in it, or see the reflection of something not visible in the room.

Nothing.

His gaze moved to the wardrobe, trying to make out the shape of the key in the lock. He had locked it as soon as he came to bed, he always did. The wardrobe was an obvious place for IT to hide. He stared at the key. Was it turning? Could IT unlock the door from the inside? Unlock the door and jump out of the wardrobe? Adrian gripped the bedding so hard his fingers started to cramp.

Nothing.

He relaxed his grip then tightened it again as his heart skipped a beat. The curtains had moved. Was that the wind or was something behind them? He replayed the vision in his mind. Had it looked like the curtains billowing out from the wind, or like something had been brushing against them? His body tensed as he waited for IT to burst through the curtains and come for him.

No, nothing.

He wished he could leap out of bed and switch the light on, but the switch was on the opposite wall. It would mean getting out of bed and putting his feet on the floor. IT would be under the bed waiting for him. He knew as soon as his toes touched the floor IT would grab his ankles and drag him under. The curtains heaved as another gust of wind rattled the window. He could feel his heart beating like a drum as he waited for the curtains to part. After a few seconds that seemed to last forever, the curtains fell back into place.

Unable to take any more, Adrian lay back down and pulled the covers over his head.

That's when he realised IT was under the covers with him.

Window In Time

It was just after noon when Margaret carried the small metal stepladder up the stairs to the storeroom on the second floor of the shop in Market Street. The wooden stairs creaked under her feet. She wrinkled her nose at the musty smell. She disliked coming up here, it always felt creepy, too many shadows and cobwebs. The paint on the walls was faded and in places had bubbled up from damp. Dust rose up from the bare floorboards as she made her way into the storeroom.

Her eyes scanned the small cardboard boxes on the shelves that lined the walls. On the top shelf, to the right of the large sash window, she saw the item she was looking for. Most stock items went straight out on display, but a selection of larger items was stored in this room. Margaret placed the stepladder in front of the shelves and opened it out. Gingerly, she climbed the steps until she stood on the top platform.

'I'm too old for this,' she grumbled to herself. 'Won't be seeing fifty again, my girl.'

Reaching up, she just managed to touch the bottom corners of the box and tickle it forward until it started to drop off the shelf.

'Won't be seeing five foot again either,' she said as she caught the box and held it against her tummy.

Just as Margaret was about to descend the steps, she glanced out through the dirty window to the upper floors of the shop on the other side of the road. Her gaze lingered. A frown creased her forehead. Something wasn't right.

The top half of the sash window was roughly square and divided into four panes. The view through three of them was as she expected: the shops on the other side of the street. However, the view through the top left pane was different. It was still the other side of the street, but not as Margaret knew it. Without thinking, she leant to the left to get a better look and nearly fell off the steps. She let out a shriek and managed to balance herself by leaning against the shelves whilst trying not to damage the box she held.

'You silly moo,' she berated herself. 'You'll give yourself a heart attack, if you don't break your neck first.'

Slowly, she stepped backwards, her right foot seeking the step below. Finding it, she shifted her balance and brought her left foot down on to the step below that, continuing until finally both feet were on solid ground and she breathed a sigh of relief. She placed the box on the floor then moved the steps until they were directly below the window. Then, using the shelves for balance, she climbed back up the stepladder. Taking the paper tissue that she kept tucked in the sleeve of her blouse, she wiped the grimy glass of the top left pane and looked through it.

The first and second floors of the buildings opposite were the same as what was currently there, albeit painted with different colours. The ground floor shop fronts were very different. Some of them had steeply angled awnings that blocked her view of the shop windows. Of the shop fronts she could see, one had dozens of pairs of dark coloured shoes hanging from the shop front. On the wall above the shop was a large wooden sign with "OLIVER'S" painted on it. Three signs hung above the shop front stating: "Largest retailer of shoes in the world". The shop next to that had an ornate wrought iron sign above, which ran the entire width of the shop front, with ALFRED A. CARVER in gold painted letters. Inside the shop window she could see white clock faces with black roman numerals. Carver's? Hadn't her Granny Emms worked in a jewellers called Carver's? But that was way back. Back before the war.

'Everything all right, Margaret?' Mr Lord, the shop manager, shouted from the bottom of the stairs.

'Yes, just coming,' she called back, hastening down the stepladder as quickly as she dared.

She picked up the box and rushed down the stairs. As she descended the final flight, Mr Lord looked up at her with a stern expression.

'Customer is waiting, Margaret.'

'Sorry, Mr Lord. The item was on the top shelf and little titch me couldn't reach it. Had to get the stepladder.'

'Fair enough, but we mustn't keep the customers waiting too long.'

'No, Mr Lord.' She hurried past him.

Mr Lord was a good boss, firm but fair, and very much from the school of "The customer is always right". He was always very professional in his demeanour. Margaret pondered mentioning what she had seen through the window but wasn't sure how he would react. She decided to keep quiet for the moment.

The rush of customers popping in during their lunchbreaks kept Margaret's thoughts occupied but as they dwindled, she fretted about whether to tell someone about what she had seen. When the shop was empty of customers, she noticed Linda, the part-time assistant and youngest member of staff, ask Mr Lord if it was okay to take a break.

'Of course, Linda,' he said.

Linda was eighteen and studying at college but worked in the shop two days a week. A sweet-natured and lively girl who was a favourite with all the staff. Margaret headed over towards the door to the back of the shop and intercepted her.

'Linda, my love, do us a favour will you?'

'What's up, Marge?' Linda tucked her shoulder length brown hair behind her ears.

'Pop up to the storeroom and take a look out of the top left pane of the window by the stepladder, will you?'

'Why's that?'

'Rather not say. You'll think I'm losing the plot.'

Linda placed the palms of her hands on her cheeks and

opened her green eyes wide in mock horror. 'Plot? There's a plot? I thought we were just making it up as we went along.'

Margaret laughed 'Get on with you, you cheeky minx. Just have a look, please, will you?'

'For you, Marge…' Linda grinned and headed for the storeroom.

While she waited, Margaret moved to the middle of the shop floor and gazed through the open doorway to the shops opposite. Everything looked normal enough.

A few minutes later Linda reappeared, her face as white as a sheet.

'Marge. The window. It's, it's…' Linda waved her hands about in front of her trying to find the words.

'Different?' Relief flooded Margaret. She wasn't going mad after all.

Linda was nodding vigorously. 'What is it, Marge? I don't….'

'It looks to me like a long time ago, before the second world war. Might even before the first world war.'

'But how?'

Margaret shook her head. 'I've no idea.'

'Everything all right, Linda?' Mr Lord said, appearing behind them. 'You look like you've seen a ghost.'

'I've just had a bit of a shock,' Linda said.

'What's happened?'

Linda looked at Margaret. 'You better explain, Marge. I need to sit down for a bit.' Linda headed off upstairs.

Mr Lord looked at Margaret with one eyebrow raised.

'It's probably best if you see for yourself, Mr Lord.'

'Curious,' Mr Lord said as he stood on the stepladder looking out of the window. 'Very curious indeed.'

Margaret knew Mr Lord was not one for flights of fancy or the supernatural, so this probably put him well outside of his comfort zone. He climbed down the stepladder and turned to face Margaret, a frown on his brow.

'I have no idea what to make of it, Margaret.'

'Me neither. Mind if I have another look?'

'Go ahead, but don't linger too long. We'd better get back to work. The stock won't sell itself.'

Margaret climbed the stepladder and looked through the window. Down on the street, she saw people going about their business. Men wearing dark coloured suits and flat caps. Ladies in long skirts, white blouses and broad-brimmed hats. Further down the street, a horse pulled a cart loaded with crates. It stopped outside of a shop, and two men, both wearing white aprons, came out of the shop and helped the driver unload the crates. A young couple came out of Carver's jewellery shop, both smiling. The woman held on to the man's arm then kissed him on the cheek. Margaret wondered if Granny Emms was working in the jewellery shop at that moment.

By the end of the day, every member of staff had been up to the storeroom and looked out of the window. Their reactions ranged from awe to utter disbelief. When the shop closed for the day, Mr Lord called all the staff together.

'I think it's probably best if we keep quiet about, err, things upstairs. We don't want word getting out, otherwise people might think we're mad.'

Linda giggled.

'Yes, Linda, I know you don't have to be mad to work here but it helps. Well, let's not give proof to that theory.'

Mr Lord's words must have gone unnoticed by some of the staff because the next morning there was a steady stream of people coming in to the shop asking about the window and if they could have a look. Mr Lord firmly but politely fended them off, citing reasons of security and safety. Just after lunch, when a large crowd of people had gathered in the shop, an overeager reporter from the local newspaper tried to sneak out to the back. The first Margaret knew about it was when Mr Lord emerged from the back frogmarching the complaining reporter by his jacket collar.

'Get off me,' the reporter said. 'I'll have you for assault.'

A gap opened in the crowd and Mr Lord marched him purposely through it.

'And I will have you for trespass. Think yourself lucky that I'm throwing you out by the scruff of the neck and not kicking you out by the seat of your pants.'

With that, he gave the reporter a shove that sent him sprawling out on to the street, causing the crowd outside to swiftly move out of the way.

'This is intolerable.' Mr Lord turned to face the crowd in the shop. 'If anyone is here because of some rumour or gossip they have heard then I would politely ask you to leave, now.'

All but three people made their way out of the shop.

'Margaret, lock the doors, and as soon as these customers have been attended to, put the closed sign up. I need to make some phone calls.' With that he disappeared out the back.

About ten minutes later he reappeared, and shortly after, a police car pulled up outside. Two bobbies got out and started to disperse the crowd hanging around on the pavement. Mr Lord took down the closed sign, opened the shop doors, and went out to talk with the police officers.

Within the hour, a van pulled up outside with ladders on top and Trevelyan Builders painted on its side. Mr Lord went out to greet the two men who got out of it. Margaret watched as he pointed up to the window then came inside with Mr Trevelyan following. The other man started taking a ladder off the van.

'Margaret, you're in charge,' Mr Lord said. 'I'll be up in the storeroom. There's a policeman out in the street should you need him.'

'Okie dokie, Mr Lord.'

The shop resumed its normal flow of customers as the afternoon went by. Just after five o'clock, Mr Lord and Mr Trevelyan came back down into the now empty shop. They said their goodbyes and the builder left.

'Right, everyone, I think we've earned the right to close a few minutes early today. Margaret, would you lock the doors please while I start cashing up?'

When all was done, and everyone was ready to leave, he called all the staff together. 'Well that was a day, the like of which I'd rather not have to go through ever again. The window-pane has been replaced, and the view out of it is now as it should be. Hopefully, that will be the end of the matter. See you all tomorrow.'

The next morning, Margaret went up into the staff room to hang up her coat and bag. The smell of sour milk and stale food assaulted her sense of smell. She looked around and saw the waste bin was still full of yesterday's leftovers. Someone must have forgotten to empty it in all the excitement. She held her breath, pulled out the full bin bag and tied it up, and replaced it with a new one. Then she carried the full bag downstairs and went out of the door at the rear of the shop, which opened on to the small enclosed yard where they kept the wheelie bin. Margaret lifted the bin lid and dropped the bag in. It landed with a crack. Margaret peered into the bin. The bag had landed on a pile of broken glass. She reached in and carefully lifted out one of the larger pieces, about the size of a postcard. She held it up in front of her face and looked through it at the old stone wall that ran along the back of the property. Through the glass, the wall looked newer than normal: no ivy covered it, and the cement in-between the stones wasn't as green and crumbling. Smiling to herself, she carried the glass inside, wrapped it in some bubble wrap then went upstairs and put it in her bag.

Danse Macabre

'Do you believe what your Grampy said earlier?' Lee asked, lying on a camp bed, gazing up at the shadows on the bedroom ceiling.

'The dance mucarber thing?' Roger linked his hands behind his head and stared up at the ceiling too. 'Nah, he was just trying to scare us. It is Hallowe'en.'

As Lee thought about what Roger's Grampy had said, his gaze moved from the ceiling to the posters on Roger's bedroom wall: The Six Million Dollar Man in mid-run; this year's Liverpool football team with '1975 F.A Cup Winners' emblazoned along the bottom; a movie-theatre poster of Jaws in which the shark's teeth glowed eerily in the darkness.

Lee liked staying over at Roger's house. Roger always had the best games, toys and comics. His mum and dad were nice too; not that Lee's own mum and dad weren't nice, but Roger's parents didn't nag Roger to do his homework or tidy his room. They also let Roger and Lee stay up late at the weekend. The only thing Lee didn't like about staying at Roger's house was the cemetery directly behind it; the thought of all the dead people buried out there made him feel uneasy. The first time he'd stayed, he'd asked Roger if he was scared by the cemetery.

'Nah, Mum said everyone in the cemetery is dead, and the dead never hurt anyone.'

Roger's mum had said exactly the same words earlier that evening. As Lee lay there, he compared her words with Grampy's, and wondered who was right.

Earlier in the week, Roger's mum had said as Friday was Hallowe'en, they could have a family party. Lee could come around after school and stay over. As soon as the final bell rang at Marlborough School that Friday, Lee and Roger were out the school door and running the short distance up the hill to Roger's house, school bags bouncing on their backs. They opened the front door, dropped their bags and coats on the hall floor and headed into the kitchen where Roger's mum was preparing the food. Roger's dad appeared in the kitchen doorway, holding several turnips.

'Turnip lanterns, anyone?' he said, dumping them on the kitchen table.

'Yes please,' the boys cried.

Roger's dad cut off the tops of the turnips with a carving knife then slid the point of the knife in and out of the core of each turnip to make it easier for Roger and Lee to hollow out the pungent veg with tablespoons. Once that was done, the boys used penknives to carve triangular eyes and jagged zigzag mouths through the sides of the turnips. They cut up candles into short lengths then weighted them down in the bottom of the turnips with plasticine.

While they did that, Roger's dad brought deck chairs out from the shed and placed them around the back yard. Then, when they had finished the turnips, he carried the kitchen table out into the yard and put it under the window. His mum came out and started to load the table with a fabulous spread of crisps, freshly baked cheese straws, salted peanuts, jelly, trifle, homemade buns (iced with batwings, witches' hats and skulls) and loads of fizzy drink. There were also tins of hotdogs and packets of white rolls on the kitchen worktop.

Grampy turned up just as it was getting dark, and while Roger's mum made him a cup of tea, the rest of them ceremonially gathered in the yard to light the candles in the turnips. The flicker of the candle flames cast eerie shadows on the walls and made the turnips seem like they were alive. Lee was a bit nervous about being so close to the cemetery, and avoided looking at it, but his fears were soon forgotten as

Roger's mum said,

'Right everyone, tuck in. And I don't want to see any food left over.'

Everyone grabbed an empty plate, loaded it up with food, filled the plastic beakers with drink (the boys had Coke, Roger's mum had lemonade, and his dad had what he called 'shandy') and then sat down to gorge themselves. When Roger's mum had finished her plate of food, she went into the kitchen to prepare the hotdogs, and was soon bringing out plate after plate of steaming, ketchup-smothered delights, the savoury aroma intoxicating. They ate in silence, except for occasional 'mmmm's' and 'aaah's' of pleasure. When all the food was eaten, and they sat there stuffed to the gills, Roger's dad started with the corny jokes.

'Did you know the cemetery is the dead centre of Falmouth.' He laughed at his own joke, but everyone else groaned. 'Everyone is dying to get in there.' More groans.

Roger's dad laughed again and took a swig of his shandy.

Lee had forgotten all about the cemetery behind him until Roger's dad mentioned it. Tingles ran down his neck as he instinctively looked in that direction, but only darkness was visible beyond the chain-link fence that bordered the cemetery.

Roger's mum stood up. 'I think I'll go and wash the dishes. If I stay here, I might split my sides with laughter.'

Thankfully, Roger's dad's supply of jokes was limited, and conversation was soon resumed.

'How're things at school, Roger?' Grampy asked.

'Got A in English this week, and a B plus in maths.'

'Well done, my lad. If you can read, write, and do your sums, anything is possible.'

'Yeah, wouldn't mind being a scientist when I grow up. Build satellites and do stuff like they do at Goonhilly.'

Listening to Roger talk so confidently about how he saw his future, Lee envied his friend. He had no idea what he wanted to do. Had no idea what, if anything, he'd be good at.

Roger's dad stood up. 'Think I'll go see if Mum needs a

hand. I'll grab another shandy while I'm at it.'

Lee and Roger glanced at each other and smirked at the word shandy. Roger's dad's voice had slurred as he said it, and Lee noted the wobble in his legs as he moved.

'You want one, Grampy?' Roger's dad called over his shoulder.

'I wouldn't say no to another cup o' tea.'

'Coming right up. You boys want anything?'

'No thanks,' the boys said in unison.

As soon as Roger's dad had disappeared into the house, Grampy fixed a serious gaze on the boys.

'So, do you two lads go along with all this ghostly 'allowe'en business then?'

'Nah, it's just a bit of fun,' Roger said.

'I think it's scary,' Lee said. 'What if all the ghosts do come back tonight?'

'Ah, the danse macabre,' Grampy said.

Just at that moment, Roger's mum came out with a cup of tea. 'Don't you go terrifying them boys, Grampy.' She handed him the steaming mug. 'I don't want them having nightmares. Dad's gone in to watch the telly, why don't you go in with him while the boys help me clear up?'

'I'll be in dreckly, just drink my tea first.' He raised the mug. 'Oh, 'n thanks.'

'Hmmm. Will you boys clear the table, please?' Roger's mum headed back inside.

Neither boy moved.

'What's the dance mucarbre, Grampy?' Roger said.

'Well, 'tis said that, at midnight on Hallowe'en, the spirits of the dead rise from their graves and all get together and perform a ghostly dance. Then the good spirits all go off to comfort their living relatives until dawn.'

'Why until dawn?' Roger asked.

'They have to return to their graves before the sun rises, or they will dissolve away to nothing and cease to exist at all.'

'What about the bad spirits?' Lee asked, fear in his voice.

'The bad ones go and find people to haunt. If they sees

you, and can get you to look at them, then they will torment you until dawn.'

While the boys pondered this information, Grampy took a sip of his tea, glanced left and right to check no-one else was about, then leaned towards the boys and in a hushed voice said, 'Some say that Death himself walks among them, cloaked in black and carrying a big scythe. He's on the hunt for souls to steal from the living. If he sees you, looks you in the eye, then you are his. He will swing his scythe and cleave your soul from your body. Then you too will join the danse macabre.'

'Grampy!' Roger's mum said from the kitchen doorway.

Lee and Roger jumped feet.

Grampy looked at her, his face the picture of innocence. 'What?'

'I told you not to terrify the boys.'

'We're not scared, Mum,' Roger said with a high-pitched squeak. He cleared his throat. 'Are we, Lee?'

'No,' Lee replied, absolutely terrified.

Not only might there be ghosts, but Death too? A shiver ran down his spine. It suddenly seemed very cold. Roger's mum looked at them unconvinced.

'Maybe it's time Grampy headed home to Granna, instead of sitting here filling your heads with nonsense. She'll be wondering where he is. Have you drunk your tea, Grampy?'

'Almost.'

'I'll go get your coat while you finish it. I thought I asked you boys to clear the table?'

The boys stared at Roger's mum.

'Now!'

They both leapt to their feet and started collecting empty plates from the table. Grampy drank the last of his tea, stood up, and put his mug on the table.

'Night lads. And remember, don't let them see you.' He walked past them and into the house.

The boys gathered up the last of the plates and headed into the kitchen, just as Roger's mum came back from seeing

Grampy off.

'Now don't you two go getting yourself all worked up about what Grampy was saying. If Granna finds out, she'll give him a thick ear. Everyone in the cemetery is dead, and the dead never hurt anyone' Roger's mum glanced at the kitchen clock on the wall. 'Look, it's after ten, time you two were in bed.'

As the boys headed to the stairs, over the sound of the television in the living room, they could hear Roger's dad, snoring. Just after they had cleaned their teeth, put on pyjamas, switched the light off and got into bed, they heard him staggering up the stairs with Roger's mum, who was whispering for him to be quiet.

'Have you ever seen a ghost or anything in the cemetery?' Lee asked, his gaze moving from Jaws' teeth to the curtains at the bedroom window.

Roger's dad's snores could be heard coming from the bedroom across the landing. Lee had once heard Roger's mum say that his dad's snoring could wake the dead, which was awkward when you live next to a graveyard. Roger had laughed, but Lee's stomach had felt all funny. The next time Lee stayed over at Roger's, he went to bed terrified, hoping and praying Roger's dad's snoring didn't wake up any dead people.

'Can't say that I have seen any. Shall we have a look now?'

'No.'

'Come on. It's Hallowe'en, we might get lucky tonight.' Roger kicked off his sheets and blankets, knelt on the pillows, and drew the curtains open.

'See anything?' Lee asked, despite himself.

'Nah, not much happening. Just Dracula, Frankenstein and the Werewolf heading home from the pub.'

Lee chuckled. 'You nitwit.'

'Why don't you come and have a look?'

'No thanks.'

'Come on, Lee. My Granna says if you face your fears, they can't scare you anymore. Just have a quick look.'

Lee pondered Granna's words. He'd met her before and liked her a lot. In fact, he thought she was the nicest, kindest person he had ever known. If Granna said something, then it was probably right. He took a deep breath, unzipped his sleeping bag, clambered out of it and on to the bed beside Roger. He rested his elbows on the windowsill as he gazed out into the night.

No moon shone, but light from neighbouring houses revealed a large, triangular, raised lawn, edged with kerbstones. No gravestones; they hadn't reached this far yet. Beyond that lawn, a wide pathway separated it from another raised lawn. From the light of streetlamps outside the cemetery, silhouettes of gravestones could be seen: some crosses, some slabs. A shiver ran down Lee's spine. Nothing moved in the cemetery, but in Lee's mind, every unrecognised shape was something terrible waiting to get him.

The nearest row of gravestones didn't go all the way across the lawn. After the last one in the row, Lee made out a darkness that he struggled to make sense of. Was it a mound? Was it a hole?

'What's that down there by the last gravestone?' he said, pointing.

Roger looked. 'That's a new grave that's been dug. Guess somebody died.'

Lee wondered if the grave was deep enough to stop the dead person from getting out after they had been buried. 'How deep do they dig graves?'

'No idea.' Roger paused for a few seconds, then said, 'Why don't we go and have a look. Find out?'

'What? No way.'

'Come on. It'll be fun.'

'What if the ghosts turn up?'

'You can see there aren't any ghosts. And anyway, it's only...' Roger looked at his wristwatch. 'Half past eleven. No ghosts 'til midnight, remember? We can be over there and back in bed in less than ten minutes.'

'But we're wearing pyjamas,' Lee said, desperately trying think of reasons not to go.

'That's okay, we can put shoes and coats on.'

'We might wake your parents.'

'Hardly. A plane could land on the roof and Dad wouldn't notice, and I'm pretty sure Mum stuffs tissues in her ears to block out Dad's snoring. Come on, let's go while we got time.'

'First sign of anything scary, we come back. Deal?'

'Deal.'

'Straight there and straight back?'

'Honest, promise. Now get your shoes on.'

They put on their shoes, headed downstairs, and took their coats off the coat hooks, where Roger's mum had hung them earlier. Roger grabbed a torch from the kitchen drawer, glanced at his watch, and opened the back door.

'Twenty-five to twelve. Still plenty of time. Ready?'

Lee's stomach did a triple back-flip. 'I suppose so.'

Roger led Lee to the left corner of the garden, where the washing-line pole and a sloping support on the fence post made for an easier climb over the fence.

'How do we get back in?' Lee asked, eyeing the fence.

'Same way. You can just get your shoe through the fence enough to rest on the sloping bit, then grab the pole and upsadaisy, over you go.'

They made their way over to the new grave, Lee's gaze constantly darting around the cemetery. Every shape and shadow increased his unease. As they reached the grave, he noticed there was a large pile of earth to the side of it.

'That's a lot of earth,' he said.

'Yeah, must take ages to dig it out.' Roger shone the torch into the grave. 'Reckon that's about six foot deep.'

'Deeper than we are tall, even reaching up.'

Lee looked around the cemetery, suddenly he grabbed Roger's shoulder.

'What's that?' he cried, pointing toward the other graves.

Roger looked where he was pointing and saw light coming up from every grave, flickering like a candle in a draught; flowing and forming into shapes. Human shapes.

'Ghosts.' Roger grabbed hold of the sleeve of Lee's coat.

'You said there were no ghosts,' Lee hissed.

'I did. But those are definitely ghosts.'

Lee looked back the way they'd come. It seemed a very long way. 'Quick,' he hissed, 'we have to get back to your house.'

'No.' Roger hissed back. 'They'll see us. Remember what Grampy said. He said, "Don't let them see you."'

'Where then?' Lee's heart banged so hard in his chest the ghosts would surely hear it any second now.

'Down there.' Roger pointed. 'In the grave.'

'What? No.'

'We have to.'

Roger gripped Lee's sleeve tighter and pulled, forcing Lee to jump down with him into the grave. They landed awkwardly, pressing their hands against the earth walls to steady themselves.

'Lie face down,' Roger instructed, turning the torch off. 'And don't look. Whatever happens.'

They lay down, side by side, foreheads resting on forearms to allow them to breathe. Lee's heart pounded, pumping fear through his veins. He could feel each ghostly presence as it slowly drifted over the open grave. Some ghosts had a sense of sadness and longing about them, others just felt like emptiness. A very few felt bad. Terrified thoughts rushed through Lee's mind. What if one of them noticed them lying there? What if a bad ghost saw them and decided to push the pile of earth in on them? Could ghosts move earth? His mind pictured a ghost laughing hideously as it pushed the pile of earth down on them in one go. Buried alive! This last thought was edged out by another - he couldn't sense the ghosts passing overhead any more.

He lay there for a few moments to confirm his thought,

and was about to tell Roger, who didn't appear to have noticed yet, when he sensed something else. Something was coming but not a ghost. This something was much worse. Lee felt the temperature drop rapidly. He shivered and heard a tinkling sound as the water froze in the earth walls of the grave. Something was at the grave and it knew they were down there.

Waves of icy cold rolled over Lee and forced their way into his thoughts; a wordless voice that urged him to turn and look up. He fought against it. 'Don't look,' he chanted over and over in his mind.

He felt Roger move beside him. Was Roger about to turn and look? He nudged his hip against Roger's and whispered, 'Don't look,' over and over.

Roger got the message, and after a few seconds he joined in with the chant.

Lee lost all sense of time as he lay there chanting, but eventually it appeared to work. The wordless voice and the icy cold receded, followed by the sense of something moving away.

Roger stopped the chant. 'I think it's gone.'

'Shall we look?'

'What if it's not?' Roger hissed. 'What if it's still there?'

'We have to look sometime,' Lee said. 'And I can't feel it anymore. It's gone.'

'Okay,' Roger said, his voice still a whisper. 'After three. One, two, three.'

They both rolled over and looked up to darkness framed by the grave.

'We should get out of here before whatever the heck that was comes back,' Lee said.

'Comes back?'

'Remember, your Grampy said they had to be back before dawn?'

'Right.' Roger stood up. 'You give me a leg up and I'll climb out, then you run and jump, and I'll grab you and pull you out. The corner's probably the best place to try.'

Lee leant against an end wall and linked his fingers into a cup. Roger placed his right foot in it and said, 'After three. One, two, three.' On three, Roger leapt up, pushing against Lee's cupped fingers. Lee braced against the strain then pulled up with all his strength. Roger was propelled out far enough that only his lower legs were over the grave.

He quickly stood, turned and crouched at the corner or the grave.

'Your turn. Take a run, grab my wrists when you jump, then try to run up the walls, okay?'

'Got it.' Lee backed up to the opposite corner, pressed against the walls then pushed off into a run then a leap. His right foot hit the wall just as Roger grabbed his wrists. He managed to grasp Roger's wrists as Roger pushed up from his squat and shot backwards, pulling Lee with him. Roger ended up sprawled on the ground, with Lee lying on top of him.

'You okay Roger?'

'No mate,' he gasped 'I've got this terrible crushing pain all down my front.'

'Oh my god? What is it?'

'You, ya dimwit. You can get off me, if ya like.'

'Sorry.' Lee clambered off, stood up and helped Roger to his feet.

'What time is it, Roger?

Roger looked at his watch. 'Jeez! It's half past six.'

Lee grabbed Roger's arm and then pointed to the horizon.

The sky was getting lighter and pale figures had started to appear.

'Quick, run.'

They fled towards Roger's house. Lee stumbled, but Roger steadied him. They jumped over the garden fence. Lee glanced back and saw there were ghosts where they had stood moments before they shot indoors.

They stood in the hallway, panting. 'That other thing, Lee said, "after the ghosts. Do you think that was...'

'...Death, yeah.'

'And we beat it.'

'You did, you mean.'

'Me?'

'Yeah. I was about to turn and look when you nudged me. You're the one who managed to keep a cool head and talk me out of it. You saved my life, Lee.'

'Dunno 'bout that.' Lee felt his cheeks grow hot.

'I do,' Roger said. 'Nobody I'd rather by my side in a crisis than you, mate.'

Lee laughed. 'Well, at least I'm not scared of ghosts anymore.'

'After dealing with Death, ghosts don't seem so terrifying, do they?'

'Nope'

'Nothing scarier than Death.'

'Hmmmm. Maybe your mum, when she sees the state of our pyjamas?

Falmouth Thirteen

Printed in Great Britain
by Amazon

41399284R00078